THE WAGGING TONGUE

Summer Edition
All the news you *have* to know!

The season is beginning to wind down in the Hamptons. But don't worry, at the Bridgehampton Polo Club there is still plenty of heat left in the summer.

We all know that the infamous **Vanessa Hughes** did her share of partying years ago. But is it true that this overindulged daughter of the polo club's owner had an affair with Argentinean polo player **Nicolas Valera**? He certainly seems to want to get closer to her again. We can't wait to see what happens.

And it seems someone is desperately trying to hush up another scandal. Known by all to be the ultimate good girl, **Brittney Hannon** may have surprised us all. For when a certain hot hunk by the name of **Connor Stone** met her on the polo field, he couldn't keep his hands off her. He's claiming to be her fiancé...but honey, where's the ring?

CATHERINE MANN

USA TODAY bestselling author Catherine Mann resides on a sunny Florida beach with her military flyboy husband and their four children. Although after nine moves in more than twenty years, she hasn't given away her winter gear! With more than thirty-five books in print, she has also celebrated wins for both a RITA® Award and a Booksellers' Best Award. A former theater-school director and university teacher, she graduated with a master's degree in theater from UNC-Greensboro and a bachelor's degree in fine arts from the College of Charleston. Catherine enjoys hearing from readers and chatting on her message board—thanks to the wonders of the wireless Internet that allows her to cybernetwork with her laptop by the water! To learn more about her work, visit her Web site, www.CatherineMann.com, or reach her by snail mail at P.O. Box 6065, Navarre, FL 32566.

EMILY McKAY

has been reading romance novels since she was eleven years old. Her first Harlequin Romance novel came free in a box of Hefty garbage bags. She has been reading and loving romance novels ever since. She lives in Texas with her husband, her two kids, too many pets and a keeper shelf that has taken over most of her upstairs. Her books have been finalists for RWA's Golden Heart Award, the Write Touch Readers' Award, the Gayle Wilson Award of Excellence and RWA's RITA® Awards. She is an *RT Book Reviews* Career Achievement nominee. To learn more visit her at www.JauntyQuills.com or at her Web site, www.EmilyMcKay.com.

CATHERINE MANN
&
EMILY McKAY

WINNING IT ALL

Published by Silhouette Books
America's Publisher of Contemporary Romance

SILHOUETTE BOOKS

ISBN-13: 978-0-373-73044-5

WINNING IT ALL

Copyright © 2010 by Harlequin Books S.A.

The publisher acknowledges the copyright holders of the individual works as follows:

PREGNANT WITH THE PLAYBOY'S BABY
Copyright © 2010 by Harlequin Books S.A.
Catherine Mann is acknowledged as the author of "Pregnant with the Playboy's Baby."

HIS ACCIDENTAL FIANCÉE
Copyright © 2010 by Harlequin Books S.A.
Emily McKay is acknowledged as the author of "His Accidental Fiancée."

Recycling programs for this product may not exist in your area.

Visit Silhouette Books at www.eHarlequin.com

Printed in U.S.A.

CONTENTS

Dear Reader,

There's nothing like a warm summer night to spark high-stakes romance! From June through August 2010, Silhouette Desire is running a new continuity miniseries—six romance-packed stories in three volumes. Escape with us to the glamorous celebrity playground of the Hamptons in A SUMMER FOR SCANDAL.

This month, *USA TODAY* bestselling author Catherine Mann teams up with Emily McKay for the third and final installment, *Winning It All* (#2031).

We hope you've enjoyed the previous books in A SUMMER FOR SCANDAL—June's *Secrets, Lies... and Seduction* (#2019) and July's *In Too Deep* (#2025). These romances are the perfect summer getaway— powerful, passionate and provocative!

Krista Stroever
Senior Editor

PREGNANT WITH THE PLAYBOY'S BABY

CATHERINE MANN

To my incredible editor, Krista Stroever,
and her amazing assistant, Shana Smith.
Thank you both for making my job a joy!

Prologue

Two Months Ago
Seven Oaks Farm, Bridgehampton, NY

"I told you to stay the hell away from my sister!"

The growled threat from her brother rumbled over Vanessa Hughes's ears a second before her Argentinean lover blocked the fist coming toward his chin.

Damn. She'd landed in the middle of a mess. Again. No surprise, since she'd always been the official family screwup. And now, she'd dragged polo player Nicolas Valera into her chaos for the second time in a year.

"Stand down, Hughes," Nicolas warned, his accent thickening. Desire and sweat still slicked her skin from their steamy encounter. Thank goodness they'd picked up their hastily discarded clothes and dressed again rather than risk being seen together in towels or robes.

Nicolas tucked Vanessa firmly behind him and faced her

pissed-off brother, Sebastian, who'd somehow found out about their surprise encounter. A feat in and of itself, since neither she nor Nicolas had planned on bumping into each other in the sauna room at Seven Oaks Farm's lavish gym.

They certainly hadn't planned on stumbling back inside together for an impulsive hookup.

Thank goodness the place was all but deserted, with most everyone at the charity fundraiser Sebastian should have been attending, the one she'd blown off to come here, only to find Nicolas had ditched the gala as well.

Sebastian pushed forward. His gaze tracked along their hastily donned clothes, his jaw flexing. "I'm not backing off until you're no longer in Vanessa's life."

"Nicolas, look out!" she interjected, hoping to forestall another blow.

Nicolas raised his forearm to block the punch. Vanessa could hardly blame Sebastian. He was right, after all. They had been doing exactly what her brother suspected, even though she and Nicolas had broken up a year ago, bitterly and publicly.

Again, her fault. Her mess.

Pivoting, Nicolas flattened Sebastian against the wooden wall with the speed and agility expected given his world-class reputation on the polo fields. He had her brother pinned with an arm across the chest, but Nicolas wouldn't be able to use his athlete's edge indefinitely. Sebastian's forehead throbbed with an angry vein.

"Calm down, Hughes," Nicolas said quietly again. Of course, he never lost his control. Except during sex. "We do not want a scene here, especially with your sister involved. Vanessa, close the door, please."

She shut the door softly.

Given that the Hughes family's Bridgehampton Polo Club sponsored the polo season at the Seven Oaks Farm, it was considered bad form for her to date any of the players. She'd made plenty of mistakes in her life, but she'd made that particular error only once before, with Nicolas.

After their breakup last year, she'd sworn never again. Until she saw him. Tonight. On the worst day of her life, when she'd been at her weakest. Not that she was renowned for demure restraint even on her best day.

Her brother stared at Nicolas with steely determination. She and Sebastian were alike in that at least, even though they didn't resemble each other, with her being the only blue-eyed blonde in her family. And oh, God, how it hurt to think about that. How it hurt to know her parents had lied to her—

Sebastian pushed free abruptly, his tuxedo tie knocked askew. "Stay the hell away from my sister, Valera." The two men faced off. "Or I swear, I'll bury you."

Vanessa tamped down bitter tears and slid between the two battling bundles of testosterone. "Oh, cut the drama, Seb. There's no law that says I can't see him. Besides, I'm twenty-five years old. It's my business who I choose to spend my time with. I don't appreciate your following after me like I'm some underage kid."

She stomped her foot, tangling it in a discarded towel she and Nicolas had left behind.

Sebastian cursed softly and grasped her arm. "There are plenty of things that aren't against the law that you still shouldn't do. Nessa, if you won't look after yourself, you leave me no choice but to intervene for your own good. I'm taking you home—"

"Hughes," Nicolas growled, his chest expanded, his onyx eyes narrowing. "I cannot just turn away, not until I am certain Vanessa is safe. So listen to me carefully. Let. Her. Go."

She winced. Talk about fuel tossed on a fire in a room already heavy with heat. She wasn't sure she could deal with this, too, not while she was still so off balance from coming face-to-face with Nicolas again, with the scent of him still all around her, the feel of his touch still tingling along her skin.

Sebastian stared down his nose at Nicolas. "Don't you dare insinuate I would harm a hair on Nessa's head. You're the one who's hurting her, cruising back into her life when you know damn well you have no intention of staying."

Her brother was right, but it smarted all the same how he blithely assumed no man would want to stick around for the long haul with her. She shrugged off her wounded feelings and focused on the combustible situation in front of her. Nobody had come to investigate the ruckus thus far, but she couldn't count on that much longer. She needed to end this confrontation ASAP.

Her eyes trained on Nicolas, she saw him trample the urge to let the fight play through. Just a flash of emotion, and then his face was impassive again.

"Your sister and I still have some things to discuss. We're all adults here." He gestured to the door. "If you would step outside."

Sebastian stepped in front of Vanessa, tucking her behind him protectively. "My sister may be twenty-five, but she has never in any way acted remotely like an adult."

"Hello?" Angry, hurt and about to lose control, Vanessa waved her hand in front of her brother's face. "Your sister happens to be standing right here, in case you didn't notice."

"Believe me," Seb said, lasering her with a censoring stare, "I noticed."

"Then let's talk about this later," she said soothingly, desperate to pacify him long enough to buy them all time to cool down. "I need to say good-night to Nicolas first, without you glaring at us."

Sebastian's face lightened for the first time. He cupped her elbow. "After the scene you two caused last year, don't you think you've had enough playing with fire?"

She squeezed her brother's arm to soften her words. "That's not your call to make."

The polo world had been stunned by Nicolas's liaison with such a flamboyant woman. Her polo-champ lover had a reputation for complete, cool control, whether on the field or in front of camera shoots for sportswear endorsements. Vanessa was anything but cool and in control.

Her brother's face hardened again into that of a calculating businessman. "As long as what you do affects our father and the reputation of the Bridgehampton Polo Club, that makes it my call. I'm the one running the family's business interests in his place. And I'm the one who'll be picking up the pieces of your wreckage."

Vanessa gasped at her brother's low blow, her skin burning as the blood drained away. Their father had cancer and was very likely dying. She might be known as the drama queen in the Hughes clan, but today had doled out even more than she could take. She swayed, growing light-headed.

Nicolas touched her back, his hand calming and exciting all at once. "Nobody wants the fallout from a scene now or anytime. Your family's reputation will be safe. Your father can rest easy."

Glancing at Nicolas's stony features, she found no sign of emotion, not even a hint of the passionate lover of a half hour ago. That shouldn't sting, but God, it did.

She turned back to Sebastian. "Nicolas and I broke up a year ago and nothing that happened here changes that."

Her brother studied her intently—she had lied often enough in the past to sneak past the constraints of her family rules—then nodded curtly. "I've said what needed to be said, Valera." He straightened his tux tie. "And Nessa? We'll talk tomorrow when we're both calmer. You owe our father peace this summer."

She bristled at the arrogance of Sebastian advising her on how to please their dad, ready to tell him as much. But he left, taking the anger and outrage with him. Vanessa deflated enough to realize he was right. She couldn't afford to follow her impulses the way she normally would. She couldn't say to hell with the world and be her regular headline-making "celebutante" self—not now.

No matter what lies her father had told her, he'd still been her rock for twenty-five years. She owed him a headline-free season.

The sound of the door closing firmly echoed. Sebastian was gone. She was alone in the spa with Nicolas for a second time.

The bench beckoned. But the weight of what they'd done washed over her. She'd actually had sex with him again— steamy, impulsive sex that left her stunned and a little bit aghast. Not that she had a clue what he felt. Ever.

Where would they go from here?

Nicolas stuffed his hands in his pockets, his eyes as dark as the black clothes he always wore. "I am sorry about your father's illness."

Weighing her words, she allowed herself a moment just to look at her enigmatic lover. She hadn't spent much time looking earlier, simply touching, tasting, savoring. *Nicolas.*

At thirty-two, he was seven years older than her, and according to the tabloids, far more mature. Leanly fit with muscular shoulders and arms to die for, he filled the room with his magnetic good looks as much as his honed size. His deeply tanned complexion attested to the hours he spent outdoors riding and training. He wore his ebony hair wavy and not quite long enough for a ponytail, just enough to appear bedroom-mussed. Thicker in front, it tended to fall over one eye. With a toss of his head, he cleared it off his forehead and turned away.

That was it? He was leaving? He took reserved to a whole new level.

Nicolas clasped the doorknob. Stunned, she opened and closed her mouth twice before speaking.

"That's all?" Rage bubbled along with frustrated tears as she kicked a damp towel aside. "You're walking out after what just happened?"

Slowly, he turned, his black shirt showcasing his too-damn-perfect shoulders in a way she refused to let distract her.

He spread his hands, palms and fingers callused from handling horses and mallets. "What do you want, Vanessa? You made it clear to your brother we are through. This was a chance encounter, a fluke, a bit of unfinished business from last season perhaps. Because God knows, you made it clear we were through to the whole world then, on national television, no less. You even accused me of cheating on you, which we both know wasn't true."

She winced at the memory of the scene she'd caused on the polo field during the stomping of the divots. Blogs had been ablaze with photos and stories. They'd even been the opening segment of cable TV's *Celeb Tonight*. She'd been running scared then. The same fear squeezed her gut now, fear of how deeply he moved her, of how badly she could be hurt. She'd run then rather than take the risk. What would she do now? "I've never had any self-control when it comes to you. And after a day like this…"

His forehead furrowed, his first real show of emotion since he'd pressed his face into her neck after they'd climaxed together. "A day like what?"

A day like this. When she'd learned she was adopted.

She could barely wrap her brain around the fact that her parents had kept her adoption a secret for twenty-five years. Her family would have continued to hide the truth if she hadn't found out by accident during discussions about whether her brother could donate blood for their father in case of emergency surgery. At first she hadn't paid much attention, since the levels of her insulin injections made her ineligible. But as she listened to the discussion of different family blood types...something wasn't right. Once the issue was raised, she'd asked too many questions to avoid the truth. At least she was the only one who knew.

And she wanted to keep it that way until she figured out how to deal with the life-changing information. But she had to do it soon, because her father—the man who'd adopted her—might not have much longer left.

After a private detective verified the truth about her adoption, she'd come to the spa to ease the confusion, not to mention the sense of betrayal. Then she'd run into Nicolas, who'd just arrived for the preseason games, and they'd fallen into old habits as fast as they'd fallen onto the sauna bench.

She pushed back the urge to haul him down with her again and forget everything for another half hour. "Does it really matter what kind of day I've had?"

"What is wrong?" His accent thickened with his persistence. He was a determined man who never gave up on the field. Although he'd sure walked away from her fast enough last year, firmly ignoring her apology.

"Drop it, Nicolas. We don't do the whole serious routine, remember? We were all about keeping it light and uncomplicated. God knows neither of us needs another scene." She drew in a shaky breath. "I can't risk worrying my father, and I know you won't risk your career."

"Except I already did that here tonight with you. As you said, we never had self-control around each other." He slid his hand into her hair, slowly, almost as if against his will.

"Something that apparently has not changed during the past year."

She stared up into his face as he loomed over, a full twelve inches taller. His eyes glinted with every bit as much desire as she felt searing her insides. Then his mouth was on hers. Heat and strength and memories—lush and intense memories of all the ways they'd pleasured each other a year ago, and again tonight—rushed through her.

Vanessa plunged her fingers into Nicolas's hair and held tight. She moaned her need against his mouth. Now, just as then, he made her forget everything but the bold brush of his tongue exploring, the feel of his hands stroking up her back, drawing her closer. She let herself slide into the convenient amnesia he offered. So unwise, so undeniable.

He eased back. "Vanessa, we can't. Not here."

Even though she knew he was right, she shook inside at the prospect of letting him go. When would she ever be able to resist him? How would she watch the games this season, watch *him* and hold strong to her promise not to bring any stress to her father's doorstep?

Her father.

The anger rose again, the betrayal of the lies he'd told her every time she asked who she looked like, since she was so different from her brother, her father, her mother. She couldn't even turn to her mother now, since Lynette had died in a car accident several years ago.

It would be easy enough to say to hell with gossip and rules, but she couldn't. Not with her father dying. There had to be a way to balance it all without combusting.

"Vanessa? Do you hear me?" Nicolas's accent stroked her like a sensuous, private promise.

And then it came to her, the perfect plan for keeping the peace in public while finally, *finally* purging this seemingly unquenchable need for Nicolas Valera.

Vanessa leaned closer, her body molding to the hard, familiar heat of him. Desire pooled low and lush. "I do hear you, and you're right. We can't continue this. Not here, anyway. But what if we pick the time and place for you to…romance me? We keep what we're feeling totally secret." *Forbidden.* "No one knows but us. Nobody gets hurt."

As she urged his head down toward her again, she could almost believe her own words. No one would get hurt…

He stopped just shy of kissing her. "You propose we have discreet sex all summer long?"

His arousal throbbed harder against her stomach.

"Not exactly." She teased his bottom lip between her teeth, trailing her fingers down his chest. "I suggest that during this polo season, you convince me, in private, that I *should* have sex with you again. If you don't succeed, then we're through. No harm, no foul. We can rest assured knowing we've learned to resist each other. And if you do succeed—" she traced his mouth with her tongue, slowly, torturously "—we'll have one helluva night to finally burn this fire out once and for all."

One

Vanessa Hughes had been burned. And it had nothing to do with the summer sun beating down overhead as she stood on the sidelines watching the polo match in action. The earth vibrated beneath her high heels from the thundering hooves passing by.

The calendar didn't lie. She was late. Scary late. Maybe pregnant late.

Her stomach bubbled with nausea. She'd forced herself to eat. She had to regulate her blood-sugar level for her diabetes, but fear had her ready to upchuck. Clamping her hand on top of her broad-brimmed hat, she peered through her overlarge sunglasses at one particular player in all black, riding his favorite chestnut sorrel.

Two months of being romanced by the intense and

passionate Nicolas Valera had been magical, soothing and stirring all at once. Although they hadn't slept together again since the sauna incident, he'd provided her much-needed distraction from confusion over learning of her adoption. Those moments of being secretly whisked away in a limo, finding anonymous flowers on her pillow, even stealing kisses in a kitchen pantry, had carried her through. She'd thought she'd found the perfect solution, and she had even considered giving in to temptation and indulging in uncomplicated sex.

That was impossible now. She was ninety-nine percent sure she was pregnant. Even thinking about the possibility made her sway in her high heels. She just had to get up the nerve to take the home pregnancy test stashed in the bottom of her voluminous purse. And she would. After the match.

Thank goodness sunglasses kept her eyes from betraying her fear to the crowd around her under the large white tent—the mainstay of old-money New Yorkers, Europeans, artsy and cultured Hampton royalty mixed with a couple of Hollywood celebrities. And right beside her stood Brittney Hannon, a high-profile senator's daughter.

Vanessa fanned her face with the program booklet. Her ever-present shades enabled her to watch Nicolas undetected as he rode across the field, mallet swinging.

Maximo's coat gleamed like a shiny penny. Nicolas loved that horse, a Crillo/Thoroughbred mix. Maximo wasn't the largest, but he was absolutely fearless.

Like Nicolas.

How would he react when she told him the news? It wasn't as if they had a real relationship beyond attraction. She wasn't sure how much more upheaval she could take.

Her heart nearly cracked in two to think of her father lying to her about being adopted. He'd always been there for her before. Her mom, however, had ignored Vanessa unless cameras were present. Not so nice to think ill of the dead, but then Vanessa didn't have much experience tempering her thoughts and emotions. This whole "good girl" gig was new to her.

She'd tried her best to clean up her act this summer, for her father's sake. No more wild-child acting out in public.

Private indulgences were another matter altogether. She just couldn't stay away from Nicolas, and that could cost her big-time. Their secret affair wouldn't be so secret once her pregnancy started showing. She glared at the ever-present cameras from behind the protective shield of her sunglasses.

"Damn paparazzi," she muttered, tapping her large black sunglasses in place.

Pulling a picture-perfect smile, Brittney Hannon linked arms with Vanessa. "As I've learned the hard way, press photos are an unavoidable part of the game. Don't let them ruin the match for you."

Vanessa turned to the senator's daughter, who'd weathered a bit of scandal herself at the start of the summer. Who'd have thought she would find a kindred spirit in the conservatively dressed Brittney, who had a reputation for being the antithesis of her showgirl mother?

"Don't you ever get tired of it?" Vanessa asked. The press had splashed racy photos of Brittney and a well-known playboy, only to learn later the two were engaged. "Don't you want some privacy? It's not as if we asked to be born into this."

Brittney blinked in surprise. And no wonder. Vanessa was known for welcoming the limelight. She'd never even considered that one day she might feel differently, and she sure hadn't realized how difficult it would be to step into the shadows.

The politician's daughter shrugged an elegant shoulder. "My father has the chance to make a real difference for our country. He takes a lot of heat as a natural byproduct of the job. The least I can do is keep my nose clean and smile for the paparazzi. Besides, none of this is real. It's all just for show." The outwardly reserved woman struck a subdued pose for the cameras, dimples showing in her cheeks. She spoke quietly out of the side of her mouth as she said, "But when I get away from all this, I'm finding it easier than I expected to simply indulge in being happy."

Vanessa wasn't even sure she knew the meaning of happy. The closest she'd come was the excitement of being with Nicolas, yet even that left her hollow inside afterward. Aching. Feeling she was missing something.

Brittney tapped Vanessa's arm with a French-manicured nail. "You have some dirt on the hem of your dress."

Gasping, Vanessa looked down at her simple, white Valentino Garavani original. "Really?" She twisted to look behind her. "Where?"

"Just teasing so you'll lighten up. You never have so much as a speck on you. Now smile."

Halfway through the round of clicking cameras, halftime started. Finally, she would be closer to Nicolas.

Vanessa slid her Jimmy Choo Saba bag from her shoulder, slipped off her heels and pulled on a pair of simple flats. Waving a quick goodbye to Brittney, Vanessa tucked her strappy heels into her oversize leather purse.

Time to divot-stomp. One of her earliest memories of coming to the matches was of holding her daddy's hand and stomping down the chunks of earth churned up from the polo ponies' hooves. She would jump up and down, smashing the ground until her Mary Janes were covered in mud.

Her mother had hated how she came home dirty, her huge hair bow lopsided. Vanessa stifled a wince. She'd despised those bows that weighed a ton and pulled her ponytail back so tightly from her face that she had a headache by the end of the day.

Smile nice for the camera, Nessa.

What a pretty baby.

The only way to get her mother's attention had been to go on shopping trips or sit still for a hair brushing. Her mother touched her only during those primping routines or when posing her for the camera.

Once she'd gotten out from under Lynette Hughes's fashionista thumb, Vanessa wore white. All the time, every day. She'd already spent two lifetimes in front of a three-way mirror as her mom put together perfectly color-coordinated outfits.

No more picking or choosing for Vanessa.

These days her hair stayed straight and free in the wind, or simply sleeked back in a low ponytail. Sunglasses covered her eyes so she never had to blink back dots from camera flashes.

People called her an eccentric drama queen. She was just tired of being a baby doll.

Baby?

Her brain snagged on the word. Her breath caught in her throat as she thought of having to tell Nicolas, of ending the fragile, tantalizing truce they'd forged. And her gaze zipped right back to the only man who could have fathered her baby, if she was indeed pregnant.

Nicolas would mingle with the divot-stomping crowd at halftime, even autograph some polo balls. He was a renowned six-handicap player after all, in the top five percent of players in the world. With fans—and with her—he would be coolly reserved, as always.

They wouldn't be able to talk, according to the rules of their summer-seduction game. Normally, she would have enjoyed playing out the moment. But today, she resisted the urge to check her watch. How long before she could slip away and use the pregnancy test tucked deep in the bottom of her purse? As much as she feared the answer, she couldn't afford to wait, not with her health concerns. Her diabetes could place both her and a baby at risk. She stomped a chunk of dirt back into the ground with extra oomph and wished her fears were as easily addressed.

Tingles prickled along her arms as Nicolas approached. She could feel him, could have even sworn she caught a whiff of his signature scent on the wind, a soap-and-cologne combo that smelled enticingly of bay leaves. He drew closer. If she hadn't known by his scent, she would have been able to guess by the reaction of those around her. People slowed, their eyes fixed on her as if waiting for her to react.

Nicolas stepped alongside her, nearly shoulder to shoulder. Her fears and wants tangled up inside her until she almost lost her balance. Nicolas pressed his booted foot ever so precisely in front of her, leveling the ground, then walking past with only the barest brush of his hand against hers. He never looked at her, didn't even miss a stride even though his simple touch had set her senses on fire.

Her fist closed around the scrap of paper he'd slid into her palm. She might not yet know the specifics of what he'd written, but she knew without question she would be seeing him alone soon.

Nicolas had arranged the location for their next tryst.

Six hours later, Nicolas added a twist of lime to his sparkling water. Nothing stronger for him at tonight's party. He never drank during the season.

Even if the timing had been different, he needed to keep his mind sharp. His instincts told him he was close to his goal of getting Vanessa back into his bed. Yes, he knew one misstep could cost him the whole game, but he had hope.

He glanced at his Rolex—thirty minutes to kill at this party before ducking out to meet her at the Seven Oaks boathouse.

Bridgehampton polo season parties were always top notch. The highest of high society pulled out all the stops entertaining their friends and celebrities in for the summer. The extravagance was so far beyond his spartan upbringing in Argentina. His village could have eaten for a month off the food spread out at multiple stations. Most gatherings were fundraisers, which took the edge off some of the decadence. Between his polo earnings and sportswear endorsements, his bank balance matched that of most of the partygoers. Still, he wouldn't forget where he came from. Nicolas emptied half his high-priced water.

Tonight's benefit was for the Humane Society. Hollywood star Bella Hudson had flown out with her hotel-magnate husband—and their dogs. Bella was talking with fellow actress Carmen Atkins. The two movie stars held the press's attention for now. Nicolas took the rare free moment to look at Vanessa.

Twenty-five years old—she was young, so young with her pampered life—yet she charmed the hell out of him. The tabloids painted a party-girl picture and he'd bought into that last year, never bothering to look deeper, only thinking about their next sexual encounter. But over the past couple of months, he'd come to realize Vanessa was also smart, witty and sensitive.

Their breakup had been tumultuous last year—and tough. He'd never known he could want someone that much. Now? He couldn't even look away, much less leave. Abundant energy crackled from her petite frame, no more than five foot two inches, *if that*. She always wore high heels and still barely reached his chin.

Tonight, in her white satin dress, she was very much the

"celebutante," perfectly groomed to catch the camera's eye. For some reason he'd never learned, she always wore white and managed to stay pristinely clean whether outdoors at polo matches or under a big tent at a Humane Society fundraiser with pets on leashes all around. Since the sun had gone down, he could see her unshielded eyes, a pale blue that turned almost silver when he made love to her.

His body jolted at the mere thought of being with Vanessa. Their secretive romancing had him on edge. He clamped down the urge to simply haul her off to the nearest room. Except he couldn't afford a repeat of the scene she'd thrown last year. He needed to project a professional image, important for his dream of launching his own training camp, even someday owning his own team.

Nicolas shifted his gaze from her to the linen-draped table of food beside her and walked closer. Swiping a tiny napkin, he trained his eyes forward and spoke to Vanessa behind the cover of his raised drink. "Did you help with the party plans?"

"Why would you say that?" She also kept her attention forward, her gaze not even straying his way as she cradled a glass of sparkling water with lime—like his own drink.

He nodded lightly toward the gauzy tent. "Everything is white."

Hydrangeas rested in clear crystal containers. Mammoth flower arrangements sat on top of pristine pillars. At least a tenth of the guests had brought their pets, yet there wasn't so much as a muddy paw print marring the décor.

Smiling, Vanessa inhaled deeply. "I adore lilies and stephanotis."

A tuxedoed waiter passed, carrying a silver tray of hors d'ouevres. Nicolas popped a smoked salmon canapé in his mouth, while Vanessa reached for a portabella mushroom and herb bruschetta. Her hand shook.

Odd.

He looked from her arm up to her pale face. "Are you all right?"

"You played well today." Ignoring his question, she dabbed at the corners of her mouth, her lipstick leaving traces on her napkin.

All summer she'd made a point of leaving hidden lip prints on his body for him to find when he showered later. Yet he still hadn't sealed the deal.

God, he couldn't wait to get her alone in the boathouse. He'd even set up a few surprises for her there. He glanced at his watch. Twenty-seven more endless minutes.

At least he could talk to her now. The *shoosh* of the champagne fountain on one side and the bubbling of the white chocolate fondue on the other added extra cover for their conversation.

She sipped her sparkling water, as the band took to the stage after their break. "I can't meet you tonight."

Surprise hit him, and disappointment, too. "You are free after this gathering, and I know it."

"Are you spying on me?"

"I just listen well enough to know you do not have plans."

"Then listen now." She placed her cup on the table. "I can't always be at your beck and call."

Surprise shifted to irritation. "You are the one who set the rules for this game."

"Sometimes rules have to change because—" Vanessa bit her lip as another waiter passed. They'd spent the whole summer brushing elbows at cocktail and garden parties, softball tournaments and music festivals, alternately ignoring each other and pretending they hated each other, while he found creative ways to pass messages for meetings. He started with simple whispered instructions of a place and time and moved on to a note scrawled on a napkin tucked into her bag.

And she'd built the anticipation well. His need for her... there were no words to express the exquisite pain. But for her to cut him off at the knees now? He wasn't sure what game she was playing. Of course while Vanessa may have been behaving in public for once in her life, in private she personified unpredictability.

Perhaps it was time for him to turn the tables. He eyed the other guests and found the partiers gathering around the stage to dance and sing along to a chorus of "Who Let the Dogs Out."

He clasped Vanessa's wrist and tugged her deftly behind a trailing gauze curtain. He pulled her into his arms and kissed her, hard and fast. She gasped, but didn't say no or push him away. She wrapped her arms around his neck. Growling deep in his throat, he delved into her mouth, sweeping, tasting sweet hints of the lime twist from her drink. He backed her deeper into the pear orchard beside the tent, an orchard that sprawled all the way to Seven Oaks. With no prior planning for this rendezvous, he followed his gut and what he remembered of the estate from last year's fundraiser for the troops.

She nipped his bottom lip, then traced the sting with the warm tip of her tongue. "We should stop. What if we get caught?"

"We won't. They're all busy dancing, and it's dark over here." He tucked her deeper into the shadowy orchard, branches rustling overhead. "You said you have to leave, so let's be together now." He'd had a lot more in mind than a few stolen kisses tonight, but if that's all they could have, he would remind her of just how good things could be between them.

Vanessa panted lightly against his neck, the sweet swell of

her breasts rising and falling faster against his chest. "We can't take this all the way, Nicolas, not here. It's too big a risk."

Desire pounded through his veins, throbbing fuller, harder, lower. "All the way?"

"I didn't mean that." She shook her head, the slide of her hair along her shoulders shimmering in the starlight. "Damn it, Nicolas, you jumble my head."

"Come closer," he pulled her hips to his, "and I'll take care of your tension."

"You're arrogant."

"But you haven't walked away." He dipped his head again, stopping just short of touching her, watching, waiting.

Shadows skittered through her eyes, illuminated by the moonbeams filtering through the trees. She blinked fast, swallowed hard, then arched up to meet his mouth full on.

Her frenzy intensified. Adrenaline still surged through him from the match, from the competition, the win. And most of all, from Vanessa. Kissing her equaled the rush of scoring three goals on a muddy course in the rain. The effort and exertion and almost painful tension was worth every bit of payoff. This woman seared his senses.

She was wrong for him on all levels with her overprivileged background and her high-strung ways. She was the one person who'd ever threatened his control. He would learn, though, how to have her while keeping himself in check. He was determined. He'd pulled himself up from a poor upbringing to become one of the wealthiest and most respected athletes in the polo world. His father had been a farmer on the outskirts of Buenos Aires, their horses certainly not of polo quality, but Nicolas had felt the calling, the affinity from an early age.

Luck had played a part in the right person seeing him in a race at eight years old. Even at that age, he was already too large to be a jockey...but polo? Argentina's famed sport was a perfect fit for him. He'd nabbed a sponsor. Now his family lived in a mansion he'd purchased for them.

Yet, no matter how hard he worked, he never forgot that a fluke of fate and the largesse of people like the Hughes family had lifted him out.

Vanessa didn't have a clue. Still, that didn't keep him away from her, even knowing her volatile nature could land him back in hot water again with his sponsors. His hands roved lower, cupping her bottom, bringing her closer.

"You're addictive," he whispered against her mouth.

She laughed shakily. "You make me sound like crack."

He swept a hand through her silky hair trailing over her shoulders. "Seeing you, feeling you move, takes me higher than any drug."

"Quit with the outrageous compliments." She scratched a nail along his bristly jaw line. "You haven't seen me all day."

"I watched you from the field." He pressed her closer until she couldn't possibly miss his arousal. So close, memories of being inside her surged through him, sending his pulse galloping against his ribs.

"You were focused on the game."

"I am a master at multitasking." He ran his hand up her back to cup her face.

She swayed toward him, then froze. She clasped his wrists. "Wait, we can't do this."

"What do you mean?"

"I can't stay. I, uh…" Shadows chased through her eyes again. "I have something to do tonight."

Jealousy nipped with the strength of a horse's bite. "Then why did you come to the party?"

"To tell you personally."

Reason edged through the suspicion. If she planned to move on to some other guy, she wouldn't be here. Vanessa might be impulsive, but she'd always been honest with him. He could count on that much. If she didn't intend to see some other man, he could think of only one other reason that would make Vanessa miss a good party.

"Are you ill?" He searched her face in the dim moonlight.

Her eyes widened. "Why would you ask that?"

"The season's in full swing and you always represent your father. You look pale. Are you having trouble with your diabetes?" Not many knew about her health concerns. She hadn't even told him last year. She'd only recently divulged it to him after he'd teased her relentlessly over her refusal to share a fudge-covered dessert with him when he'd chartered a jet to fly them to dinner in a remote Vermont town last month. The isolated locale and distance from the Bridgehampton frenzy provided the anonymity they needed to enjoy an evening together.

She shook her head. "I know how to monitor myself. I've been doing it since I was nine."

After she'd set aside that uneaten sundae, Vanessa had told him about learning to overcome her fear of needles to administer her own injections as a teen. She'd vowed it hurt less than watching her father wince when he gave her the shots. She cared for her dad, that was patently obvious. Christian Hughes's battle with cancer had to be hell for Vanessa. No wonder she was moody.

Nicolas rested his forehead against hers. "You have had a stressful summer. I only want to make sure you are all right. I…care for you."

And he did care. He'd always wanted her, but somewhere around the time she'd sipped her diet soda to hide the tears over how much her father worried about her health, Nicolas had felt something shift inside him. He felt that same unsettling change rumbling around in his chest again now.

Her fingers clutched the lapels of his suit, her forehead furrowing. Something obviously weighed heavily on her mind, something that had made her want to cancel their evening rendezvous.

"Nicolas, I should tell—"

A rustling sounded through the trees, fast, loud. Vanessa jolted, her mouth snapping closed. Nicolas pivoted fast to shield her from view, because the crunch of underbrush left him with no doubts.

Someone was coming toward them.

Two

Vanessa clutched Nicolas's arm, her heart hammering as hard as the bass throb of the distant band. Frantically she scanned the shadowy clearing, peering through the surrounding trees. The underbrush rustled louder. A scruffy dog lunged from behind a pear tree.

Straight toward Vanessa.

She stifled a scream and ducked behind Nicolas. Not that she was scared of dogs, but this little beast rocketed forward at lightning speed, pink leash flapping behind. Nicolas shielded her, his stance planted. Vanessa gasped in gulping breaths to steady her pulse, the clean night air fragrant with ripening pears. The wiry-haired mutt ran circles around them, yipping, but thank heavens not nipping

"Thank heaven, it's just a dog." She rested her cheek against Nicolas's back, the scent of his bay-rum soap stirring arousing memories of showering with him last summer. But the rowdy little pet had served up a hefty reminder of how easily they could be interrupted. Discussing her possible pregnancy would require total privacy. "We can talk later. I'll just walk the dog back to the party before someone comes looking—"

A whistle echoed in the distance. "Muffin?" a female voice shouted through the night. "Muffin, come here sweetie. Come to Mama."

Rhinestone collar refracting moonbeams, Muffin's ears perked up, twitching like satellite dishes working for a better connection. She was one ugly-cute scrap of fur, and small to have made so much noise.

"Muffin?" the female voice sounded louder, closer.

Nicolas knelt to grab for the leash. Muffin scampered deftly out of reach. A branch swayed.

"Damn," Nicolas muttered. "No more time."

He gathered Vanessa tightly against his chest and guided her behind a tree. Muffin trotted toward them, all but pointing a paw their way. Vanessa's stomach clenched. They'd eluded the press, her family and Nicolas's Black Wolves teammates all summer long. They couldn't possibly be discovered now because of one persistent pup.

"Shoo, shoo!" She waved the dog away with her hand.

"Shhh," Nicolas whispered before brushing a kiss across her cheek.

Just a simple skim of his lips had her relaxing deeper into his arms, her legs more than a little wobbly.

Staying still and quiet was tough enough with Nicolas clamping a possessive hand on her spine, his fingers straying to dip inside the swooped low cut back of her silk charmeuse evening gown. The air grew thick, her breathing so raspy she feared Muffin's owner would hear. Damn Nicolas and his tormenting caresses that turned her muscles to marshmallows right when they were seconds away from possible discovery.

Who was the impulsive one now?

"Muffin," the female voice demanded, branches parting a couple of trees away, "no more playing. Come. *Now!*"

Muffin sighed heavily and turned away, trotting toward her owner, leash tracing a serpentine trail in the dust back into the trees.

"There you are," the woman said—to her dog, thank goodness. "You're a naughty girl…" Her voice faded as she left with her pet.

Vanessa sagged back against the tree trunk, ragged bark biting into her back. Her heart drummed in her ears in the quiet aftermath. "That was close."

"Too close."

His fierce scowl reminded her well how dangerous a game they played. Her liaison with him now would cause a bigger scandal, given how she'd ended things before. Her brother had been angry enough last year when rumormongers had dared impugn the Hughes family's impartiality just because she happened to be sleeping with one of the players…. Okay, her brother wasn't at fault for her decisions. She had known going in that it would look bad.

Yet, here she was again, with Nicolas. How was she any better now than last summer? Just better at deception.

Nicolas looked from the clearing back to her. "They're gone. We're safe. Now what did you want to tell me?"

A secret that would pour fertilizer onto the rumormongers. She should wait until she was sure. Why upset him for no reason? She still hadn't taken the home pregnancy test. Better wait to confirm the pregnancy. She would decide what to do then.

Vanessa smoothed his tuxedo lapels. The heat of him warmed through the fabric and tempted her to explore further. Desire crackled through her until she could have sworn her hair sparked with static, but for once she would be strong around him. "We will have to talk later. I'm not thinking clearly tonight. It was a long day in the sun. I should have skipped the party."

She *should* have skipped a lot of things this summer. But looking up into Nicolas's dark eyes melting over her like the dangerous chocolate she shouldn't have, she couldn't delude herself into thinking she was any stronger at resisting him now than she had been before.

He nodded curtly. "Okay then. No boathouse for tonight. But rest up, Vanessa, because by tomorrow I will have an even more enticing plan in place, one you can't resist." His hands slid in a seductive path from her back to her hips then back up, stopping just below her breasts. "We're going to be together soon."

His confidence would have irritated her, except she knew full well her ability to resist him was in serious peril. She would not be impulsive this time the way she'd been in their last encounter, not to mention all their assignations last year. With the possibility of a surprise pregnancy looming over her, she needed to stay in control now more than ever.

Carefully, Vanessa closed the front door of her childhood home with the barest click echoing up into the vaulted foyer. She was good at sneaking in undetected after years of practice.

The Tudor-style mansion still radiated the same formality, with bulky antiques, thick curtains and the heavy scent of lemon furniture oil. The hallway sprawled upward into a cathedral ceiling, open to the living room. Her father hadn't changed anything since Lynette died.

Vanessa grasped the banister, the wooden rail cool and familiar under her hand. Even from the stairs she could see the carved fireplace mantel with a massive oil portrait of her and Sebastian as children above. The rest of the art on the walls was polo-centric—horses in action with bold players, women in long dresses and umbrellas watching from the sidelines. She'd taken a marker to one as a child, muddying up a dress with a Sharpie.

Wow, she'd been a brat. Yet she'd never doubted her dad's love.

Once her father had gotten out of the residential treatment facility last month, she'd closed up her sleek little condo in New York City and moved back to the fourteen-bedroom family hub without even asking. Sure her dad had plenty of nurses, but she wanted to spend as much time with him as possible. She liked to think her presence comforted him, even if he didn't say so. And she could still continue her new job for the season, her pet project—increasing entertainment activities for the children of spectators. She was trying to make amends, but it was hard knowing where to turn when her world was flipped upside down.

Italian heels dangling from her fingers, she tiptoed down the hall, not wanting to wake her father. He slept so fitfully these days. Of course, he'd always been a light sleeper with an ear perked to listen for her as a teen.

"How was the party?" her father's voice called through his partially opened bedroom door.

Caught again. Had she ever fooled him at all? Her heart squeezed with love for him.

She stepped inside, hinges creaking softly. "Hi, Daddy."

Christian Hughes lay propped up by a pile of pillows in his four-poster bed. His face was chalkier than the ivory satin sheets. The thick comforter enveloped him, his body emaciated from the treatments. He seemed frail, as if the heavy bedspread could crush him like poured concrete.

He'd completely shaved his head after the second round of chemo robbed him of his freshly grown hair. He looked just like his son, Sebastian. Of course, Seb was the biological child. She swallowed down welling tears her ailing father didn't need to see.

Her father had always been fit and tanned from days on his horses, full of energy whether he was cinching million-dollar deals or stomping divots with his daughter.

Now his breathing rattled.

And her heart broke.

She stepped deeper into the muggy room, temperature cranked up because he was frequently cold. Setting her shoes and purse on the floor, she sat on the antique beech-wood chair beside his bed and tucked her legs underneath her. "Sorry to wake you."

"You didn't. I was waiting up." He raised a bony hand and patted her arm, his fingers so thin the wedding band he still wore almost slid off. "I know you're an adult, but even when you're fifty and under my roof, I will worry until I hear your feet hit the stairs."

His hand slid from her, skipping lightly along a framed family photo on the bedside table before falling to rest on the bedspread. The picture had been taken when she was around five, her sky-blue bow perfect for the start of polo season. She wasn't looking at the photographer, but rather staring off into the distance. She still remembered the day and how she'd wanted to play in the barn instead of attend a match that seemed endlessly long.

That day, she would have taken a Sharpie to the polo players' stark-white pants if there'd been one handy. Those feelings had been the driving force behind her ideas for expanding the activities offered to entertain the children of families attending polo matches. "I'm sorry I've given you reason to doubt me."

"You're high-spirited, but in a good way, like Sassy." One of his prized fillies, gone now from old age. Sassy had been past her playing prime when Vanessa was a child, but the horse still had spirit.

"Remember how I begged to ride her?"

A reminiscent smile tugged at his parched, cracked lips. "Scared the hell out of me that day I relented."

"I got tossed on my butt." She'd stained and torn her best riding pants, which had made her mom mad. Her dad had usually been able to tease Lynette out of her tempers. That day he'd been silent, shaken.

She understood the feeling too well now as she faced the possibility of losing him. "Thanks for letting me ride her."

"I never could say no to you."

"I meant thanks for letting me land on my butt. I learned more that way."

He laughed weakly. "That's my girl."

Too bad she still had to learn the hard way.

She glanced at the family photo in the silver frame. Her father had placed it there after Lynette died to remind him of his perfect family. Perfect except for Lynette's tantrums and how they'd kept a huge secret from their children. What had made them decide to adopt her? What had made her biological parents give her up?

Her hand slipped to her stomach and she thought of her own increasing nerves as each day passed on the calendar. She wasn't mother material any more than Lynette Hughes had been. Panic pounded her chest for a brief moment until she quickly realized she would never put an emotional wall up between herself and a child, no matter how different her child was from her.

Still, Lynette had chosen to bring her into this house. Why? She wanted to ask Christian, needing answers, though she couldn't make herself add another line of worry to his weary face tonight. But his frail frame reminded her time could be running out. Her answers could die with her father.... The last thought choked her.

She would hold on to her questions for a while longer.

Vanessa patted his hand, bruised from multiple IVs. "I'm glad you waited up for me so we could talk."

"I always wait up for my girl."

How many hours of worry had she caused him? Had pushing the envelope become such a habit for her she'd subconsciously chosen Nicolas to create a stir? The possibility unsettled her more than a little. Maybe, just maybe, she'd done that last year, but this year? Her attraction to him was undeniable. There was definitely no secret wish to get caught, because that would end things for him. Nicolas had been her one bright spot in a summer filled with pain.

"Vanessa?"

Her father's voice sliced into her thoughts. "I was, uh, just thinking about the party. The Reagerts always throw a fabulous bash."

"That they do. I'm sorry to have missed it, but I'm glad you were there to represent the family along with your brother." He skimmed a hand over his shaved head absently. "You've been a real comfort to me this summer. I know you'll keep the traditions alive."

"Daddy, don't talk like that." She rested her hand on top of his over his bald head and squeezed gently. "You'll be out there divot-stomping with me next year."

"I hope so, Nessa, I hope so." His eyes drifted closed, his chest rising and falling evenly.

Vanessa sat beside his bed and watched him sleep for a few minutes. How sad that she was tucking him in now, this once big, strong father who'd long ago created bedtime stories with her favorite horse puppets. Once she was sure he was resting peacefully, she slipped out into the hall to her suite. She locked the door behind her and sagged back with a ten-ton sigh.

Finally, she was alone.

Pushing away from the door with purpose, she strode toward her bed and upended her purse onto the mattress. Her shoes and wallet mixed in with a thousand other items, but her eyes zeroed in on one thing.

The home pregnancy test. A thin box would spell out her future with a plus or minus sign. Her health dictated she learn the truth soon. While she might be reckless when it came to her own safety, she couldn't risk the well-being of a baby.

Scooping up the pregnancy test, she willed her shaky hand to steady. She would know in minutes whether she was free to meet Nicolas in the morning.

Or whether she would have to make a last-minute appointment to see her doctor.

Three

Where is Vanessa?

Nicolas brushed down Maximo, each stroke faster and faster as his irritation built. She'd been a no-show this morning for their brunch date at a tucked-away inn. While she'd let him know, her format—a text message—had left him frustrated. The fact that she was ignoring his calls shifted his frustration to anger.

Even his favorite ritual in a quiet corner of the stable couldn't calm him. The scent of polished leather, hay and nature usually soothed his soul. No matter where he traveled, in a stable, he felt at home. Since he was usually on the road for polo matches or traveling to photo shoots for his sportswear endorsements, there wasn't much in the way of routine in his life. He'd made a mistake in getting comfortable with his "routine" with Vanessa this summer.

Most of their evenings were orchestrated around the parties they had to attend. So he'd made a point of surprising her with late brunches after he'd finished his morning workout with the team's owner, Sheikh Adham.

Now that he looked back, he realized she'd been disappearing more and more. He didn't expect to know her every move or thought like some possessive jackass, but he could see how distracted she was lately. Which concerned him, as well as surprised him. Their time together this summer was supposed to be about attraction, passion. Certainly last summer had been about all that, yet these past two months—with no sex—had added a need he hadn't expected. A need to know her, to figure out if he could trust this new wiser, more mature Vanessa.

Footsteps shuffled along the dusty floor behind him. He looked back over his shoulder just as Vanessa rounded the corner.

"Sorry I'm late," she said softly, her large sunglasses silver today. Her white jeans and button-down shirt hugged her body, made him think of just how fun it was to peel away those layers. "I had an unexpected appointment."

"I got your text message." He forced his focus back on her words.

She would *not* unsettle him. He couldn't afford disruptions during polo season.

So what was he doing with Vanessa at all?

"It was rude of me not to call." She slid her sunglasses on top of her head, shifting from foot to foot nervously. "I was distracted. Not that you're easily forgettable, far from it."

He set the brush aside and looked into her troubled blue eyes. His instincts itched in the same way they did on the field, when he knew his horse was off even if he showed no perceptible signs. "Something is wrong."

Her hand shook as she fidgeted with her sunglasses again. "I had to check in with my doctor."

"Are you all right?"

"Healthy as a, uh, horse."

She slid her sunglasses back over her eyes in a gesture he'd come to recognize well. She'd closed herself off. Time to move on. He wouldn't get anything more from her on that subject today. Best to advance again later.

A whinny sounded a few stalls away.

Nicolas recognized the pony's call even though it wasn't one of his. They all had distinctive "voices." It paid to know everything about the polo ponies as well as their riders on the field. "Careful around Ambrosia or she'll nip you on the butt. She's high-spirited. It'll take a while before she's ready to be played."

"Sounds like one of my dad's favorite horses—Sassy. She might have been high-strung, but she was all heart."

Like Vanessa?

The sound of Ambrosia's groom echoed around the corner as the woman crooned to the pony with an unmistakable New Zealand accent. Catherine Lawson was the head groom for Sheikh Adham ben Khaleel ben Haamed Aal Ferjani, the owner of Nicolas's team. Sheikh Adham not only owned the team, but was also one helluva top-notch player for the Black Wolves.

Vanessa's brow furrowed. "Maybe we should speak somewhere else."

Nicolas cupped her elbow. "Lawson won't be coming this way. She still has to tend Sheikh Adham's signature ponies, Aswad and Layl."

Except for Nicolas, all the Black Wolves rode Sheikh Adham's horses. Aswad and Layl, Arabic for Black and Night, came from the same sire, the Sheikh's first horse. They were solid and glossy black, damn near perfect. He saved these prized ponies for the most crucial parts of a match.

Still, Nicolas would put his money on Maximo any day of the week. He patted the polo pony's smooth neck, the mane roached—shaved—so as not to get tangled during competition.

Maximo wasn't some elite Arabian, but he was a hearty Argentinean criollo mixed with a thoroughbred for endurance and speed. All five of Nicolas's personal ponies were of the same breed, but Maximo? He was special. At fifteen hands high, he wasn't the largest on the field. Yet even with mallets flying and the largest of the large bumping him, Maximo never flinched.

Vanessa stroked the sorrel's nose with obvious affection. "Funny how we can trace their lineage further than our own."

Nicolas cocked a brow. "There are books written about the Hughes family tree."

She rubbed her cheek against Maximo without hesitation or fear. "I'm not a Hughes. I'm adopted."

Shock snapped through him harder than any nip from a horse, but he fought to shake it off fast for her sake. From the pained expression on her face, it seemed she hadn't quite made peace with the information. He searched for the right words.

He hated platitudes, so he settled for the truth. "You may not be biologically related to Christian and Sebastian, but you believe me, you are every bit a Hughes."

A smile flickered along one corner of her mouth. "I don't think you mean that as a compliment."

Damn, apparently he hadn't struck the right chord. He spoke English fluently but still missed nuances on occasion. "Sorry, I did not mean to make light of something that's obviously painful for you. How long have you known?"

"I only found out at the beginning of the summer."

Could that be the reason for her distraction lately? He wanted to haul her into his arms, but she was emitting hands-off vibes. "That must have been a shock, learning as an adult."

"That's an understatement."

"How did you find out?"

"Through Dad's treatments." She gripped the wooden stall plank until her fingers went bloodlessly white. "There was some discussion about donating blood to be stored if Christian needed transfusions. I couldn't give because of my insulin injections, but in listening to the discussions about family blood types, I started wondering. It's a lot of techno medical garble, but basically, I realized I couldn't be Christian and Lynette's biological child. I had a private detective look into it. He discovered I was adopted as an infant."

He wasn't sure why she was telling him this here, now, but she needed to talk and he couldn't deny the need to learn more about her. "What about your birth parents?"

"The detective hasn't learned that part yet, and I told him not to dig any further. What if my biological parents don't want to be found? I decided to ask my father—Christian—for any other information."

"What did he have to say?" The Christian Hughes he'd come to know over the years adored his only daughter to the point of indulgence. Surely he would have reassured her with his explanation.

She scrunched her nose. "I chickened out and never asked him. He doesn't even realize I know."

He could see the concern in her eyes for her father. She'd made a mature and thoughtful decision not to worry him. Nicolas squeezed her shoulders in quiet comfort. It wasn't just wishful thinking on his part that he was seeing a new side to this woman. She had a tender heart beneath the more impulsive instincts.

Nicolas stroked her neck with his thumbs. "You don't want to worry him while he's ill."

Last year, she hadn't given a thought to worrying her father, even when he'd been in the early stages of his battle with cancer.

"Actually, until now, I haven't even been able to discuss it with anyone." She squeezed her eyes shut for an instant, her shoulders tensing under his hands. "I was so upset when I found out, I ran out of the detective's office and came straight here to ride out my feelings. It didn't help. I was an even bigger mess. I didn't dare show my face in public, so I skipped the start-of-the-season party and went to the..." Her eyes shifted nervously.

Realization booted him as solidly as a horse's hoof to the chest. "You went to the sauna to steam away the pain and you found me."

And they'd made love in the heated enclosure, the sprawling gym all but abandoned while everyone else attended the party. Seeing her then had been a bigger shock than he'd expected. He'd prepared himself to see her on the field and had been determined to keep his distance. However, running into her when she wore only a towel, perspiration and vulnerable eyes had leveled all his best intentions.

He leaned back against the stall wall, crossing one booted foot over the other. "I wondered what made you cave in so easily after announcing to the entire world, on national television, that you wouldn't sleep with me again even if—" He held up a finger. "Now let's make sure I get this right.... Even if I was hung like the best stallion in the stable."

Unmistakable remorse flitted through her eyes. "Did I actually say that?"

"There are plenty of YouTube videos out there to document it." Damn, he'd been angry—and disappointed. He'd deluded himself into thinking the media frenzy surrounding her had been hype. Just like he was doing this year.

She rested a hand lightly on his arm, her eyes glinting with more of that contrition he wanted to believe was real. "I really am sorry for causing you embarrassment. You didn't deserve that kind of treatment."

While he wasn't sure he completely trusted her yet, he did appreciate the effort she was making now. "Thank you for the apology."

"I apologized last year, too."

"But I believe you mean it now."

Her hand rubbed lightly up and down his arm, just under the rim of his fitted black T-shirt. "You didn't say if you've forgiven me."

"I forgive you," he conceded. It was the truth, after all. Yet if he was telling the truth, more needed to be said. "I'm just not sure yet if I trust your change of attitude to last."

Vanessa's face froze into an expressionless mask—a beautiful, pale mask—until she finally nodded tightly. "Fair enough. Trust takes time. I'm not sure I trust myself to be quite honest about everything I'm thinking either."

He wanted to press her on what those other things might be, but they'd already made progress here. They weren't in bed, but they'd grown closer. She'd talked to him, shared a secret with him she hadn't told anyone else. That touched him as surely as her hand on his flesh.

Dipping his head, he brushed his mouth over hers, nothing deep or passionate. Hell, their mouths were even closed. But the feel of her lips under his, not pulling away, had a special intimacy all its own.

Easing back slowly, she squeezed his arm. "Be patient with me, okay?"

"I can do that."

Vanessa sketched her fingers over his eyebrows. "Would it help soothe the sting if I told you you're hung like the second-largest horse in the stable?"

His laughter burst free. God, he enjoyed the audacious way

she surprised him. "Tomorrow, spend the afternoon with me and we'll see."

Lucky for him, for the past few weeks he'd been working on the perfect plan to have Vanessa all to himself, no concerns about interruptions. He wanted Vanessa Hughes in his bed, even though he was quickly realizing one more time wouldn't be nearly enough.

Hooves thundered with the passing ponies. Vanessa planted her palm on her floppy hat as Nicolas's team approached the end of a short practice match. She'd considered keeping her distance but hiding seemed more conspicuous. Instead, she lounged in an Adirondack chair a few feet away from the small clusters of other observers.

The crack of a mallet connecting, the scent of earth churned under the ponies' hooves all wrapped around her with familiarity. She needed that comfort right now more than ever.

Her pregnancy test had been positive, a diagnosis the doctor confirmed. The physician had immediately recommended a high-risk OB but had assured her that while there were health concerns, she had every reason to believe she would deliver safely.

Provided she adhered to the doctor's monitoring and orders.

Equipped with prenatal vitamins, a rigid meal plan and stacks of reading material, she'd left the office—and run straight into Nicolas at the stables. Okay, so maybe she'd been hoping to run into him by showing up at the most likely place to find him. She'd needed to see him. She just wasn't ready to tell him yet. The news still hadn't settled in her mind. Polo season was almost over. Perhaps it would be best for all if she waited until then to share the news.

So here she was, seeking Nicolas out again. Dreaming of

what could have been if she hadn't screwed up so badly last summer.

Her eyes were drawn to the sleek lines of his body in motion as he swung the mallet, the way he moved as one with his horse. And most of all, she couldn't look away from his intensity. The way he poured himself into the game was mesmerizing. Much like the mesmerizing intensity he poured all over her while making love.

Would she ever feel that beauty again? He'd said he forgave her, but he still didn't trust her. How could she risk being with him when they were still missing such a fundamental element need to make a relationship work?

The sound of footsteps pulled her out of her reverie. She glanced over just as her brother drew up alongside her.

Sebastian dropped into a chair next to her, looking anything but relaxed in his business suit. "How's the practice match going?"

"They're almost through," she answered tightly. She and her brother hadn't spoken in private since the explosion at the sauna. "What brings you out here?"

"Saw you from my office window. Thought I'd stop by."

More like he was checking up on her to make sure his little sister was behaving. "I'm not stalking Nicolas, in case you were wondering. I'm simply showing my support the way Dad would want us to."

"Good, I'm glad to hear you're done with Valera."

"I'm glad you've quit punching out polo players." Well, technically he'd only punched out one. How much angrier would her brother be when he learned about the baby? Apprehension tightened her chest.

Sebastian laced his hands over his stomach. "Still mad at me, are you?"

"You behaved like a beast and you know it, not that you've

apologized. I was embarrassed and hurt by the way you acted in the sauna."

"But you obviously listened." He reached across to squeeze her shoulder. "You've really gotten your act together this summer, Nessa, and you have to know that's been a comfort to our father."

She noticed he still hadn't apologized for overreacting. She had such a short time to come to some kind of resolution with Nicolas before everything hit the fan with her family. The fear constricting her chest shifted to panic.

Vanessa pulled a tight smile. "Don't you have more important things to do than worry about my love life? Go back to work, or take your fiancée out to lunch. Scram."

Sebastian studied her through narrowed eyes before nodding curtly and standing. He started to speak again, then shook his head and walked away. Vanessa blinked back tears, wishing life wasn't so complicated. She looked back at Nicolas just as the practice match ended.

Morning sun beating down on him, Nicolas tugged his helmet off and sweat slicked his dark hair to his head. Her body ached to be near him again, but there was still so much unresolved.

Nicolas had asked her to spend the afternoon with him. Was it wise to spend time alone with him right now, while her feelings were still so raw over finding out about the pregnancy?

With time ticking away, she didn't have a choice. She had to resolve things with Nicolas one way or another before the rest of the world—and her volatile brother—found out about the baby.

Vanessa swung her feet up onto the sofa in the private railway car. Propping her chin on her hand, she stared out the tinted window as the Long Island shore whipped past. She was thrilled and entranced by Nicolas's idea to spend the afternoon together. Apparently he'd gone to a lot of trouble to arrange this in advance. That he would go to so much trouble, think so far ahead about them together, touched her heart. "How did you come up with this idea?"

Nicolas lifted her legs and sat beside her, resting her feet in his lap. "Train travel is more prevalent where I come from."

"Well, I'm totally a fan."

The sheen of polished mahogany wainscoting with a brass chandelier anchored overhead created an old-fashioned, time-away-from-the-world feel she desperately needed right now. The air was thick with the scent of orchids filling a crystal vase. White flowers. A small nod to her color preference that she couldn't help but enjoy. Antique linens covered a small table with a silver tea service at the ready.

And yet she was too nervous to enjoy it all to the full extent.

She looked away from the window, needing to focus on what was right in front of her, leaving everything else behind. The gilded mirror reflected her pale face, although she felt fine, wide awake, in fact, and all too aware of the double just beyond the archway.

Maybe she should focus on the table for two instead, where they'd shared almond chicken salad, cheese and fruit—all perfect treats to tempt her palate without risking sugar overload.

At least she could indulge her ravenous appetite. This probably wasn't the best time to indulge in sex, when her emotions were in such turmoil over the pregnancy. So far he wasn't pushing, simply rubbing her feet and talking.

The railcar rocked ever so slightly, just enough to sooth without overpowering. Exactly what she needed. And wow, he could continue that foot rub forever. "What an amazing idea."

"You inspire me." The words rolled off his tongue with a thicker accent than normal, one of the few indications of emotion from her stark lover.

"What a beautiful thing to say."

He paused his massage, his hands simply holding her feet. "Beautiful?"

"Don't get your testosterone in a twist. You're totally masculine, almost too much so sometimes. Be thankful you have that sexy accent to add a romantic edge to the 'oozing machismo.' I do believe that's the phrase I saw in a recent tabloid piece on you."

"You've been reading up on me, 'Fearless Vanessa'?"

She clamped her hands over her ears. "I hate that headline."

He rested his hands over hers and linked their fingers until she slid into his arms. "Vanessa," he said, his voice caressing her ears as surely as his thumbs stroking her wrists, "it's true. You have an unconquerable spirit."

"Spoiled, you mean," she said with a wince, remembering an old accusation.

He held her eyes with his, so dark, mocha-rich and mysterious. "I'm sorry for not taking the time to get to know you better last year."

"We were kinda busy with other pastimes."

Memories swirled between them—sex in the shower, in the stable, in her car, anytime the mood stirred...and it had stirred so very often. How strange this celibate summer was in contrast.

Slipping her hands from his, she crossed her arms over her stomach as if she could somehow hold on to her secret, on to this understanding between them, longer. "I'm a master at dodging the press when I wish, but even I never knew there were this many places to hide. You've outdone yourself these past couple of months."

"I see your world differently than you do."

"What do you mean?"

His thumb worked along the tender arch of her foot. "You've walked the path so often you see what you expect."

A shiver of awareness sparked from her foot upward. "You know all about my life here, but you never talk about growing up."

"As you said, we were too busy to talk much last summer." His thumbs worked with such seductive precision she began to wonder if the sensual massage was part of some grander plan.

"The way we handled things was a mistake."

"Perhaps." He worked along one toe at a time.

She swallowed hard, her body languid. How could she be so relaxed and turned on all at once? "Talk to me now, about your childhood."

"Pfft," he dismissed her question. "You can read my bio on Wikipedia the same as anyone else can."

"And of course I already have." She refused to be distracted that easily. This was her chance to ask more, to be more. "Wiki doesn't tell me about your paths."

"I'm a fairly uncomplicated man. My family wasn't wealthy, but we weren't hungry. My sisters and I had what we needed. I lucked into a chance to increase the family coffers, and I took it."

He said it all so simply, sparse with his words and emotions. She knew there was more to him, even if he offered few glimpses behind his impassive mask.

Regardless, she refused to let him dismiss his impressive accomplishments. "My father says the harder he works, the luckier he gets."

A rare smile twitched his seductive mouth. "I like the way your father thinks."

"I believe you look at paths and see opportunities."

"If it makes you happy to analyze me, feel free." His hands slid up to her ankles, clearly intent on distracting her.

"Am I an opportunity?"

"Woman, you are a walking, talking, mesmerizing liability, and you damn well know it." His fingers worked along muscles up to her knees, his hands hot and strong and tempting even through her jeans.

She clamped his wrists and stopped his path. "I think I'm insulted."

He held her hands and met her eyes again with intensity and even a hint of anger. "You slapped me in front of a dozen reporters—and your family. Such a huge crowd gathered to gawk, the other game had to be stopped. A senator and a visiting ambassador left—conspicuously, I might add. I don't know about you, but that is most certainly not the professional face I wish to display."

The power of his emotions stirred her own. He might be mad, but she knew he would never hurt her. In fact, he was so gentle with her sometimes she wanted to rattle him and shake free the powerful passion she knew they shared. "You shouldn't have called me a spoiled and immature princess."

"You shouldn't have acted like one."

The immature part had stung most, and still did. But she had to accept that she'd earned that reputation. Repairing the damage and regaining trust was her responsibility.

She was trying to make amends, but time was ticking away so fast for her this summer. She didn't know how much longer she would have with Nicolas. Who knew how he would react when he learned about the baby? Would he consider this yet another reason he couldn't trust her? But could she help it if she wanted to get closer to him, to earn back his trust before news of the baby weighed into his thinking? Either way, she could lose him altogether, and it hurt to think about a lifetime of wanting him.

Right now could be all she—they—had.

Decision made, Vanessa knelt beside him on the sofa, linking her arms around his neck. Before she could lean in to kiss him, Nicolas swept her up with the predatory growl she remembered well.

Months of waiting was about to end.

Four

His waiting had come to an end. Finally, he had Vanessa back in his bed. Or in this case, in the bed in his railcar, once he carried her from the parlor compartment through the archway to the bedroom.

He sensed the difference in her kiss, the subtle suggestive pressure of her mouth. Testing his perception, Nicolas traced her pouty bottom lip with his tongue, and she opened immediately. The taste of melon and cheese, Vanessa and him, mingled in a foreshadowing of the deeper connection they would share soon. But not too soon. He wanted to draw this out for her, ensuring an encore.

Nicolas settled her on the plaid spread piled high with decorative pillows and shams. The mattress dipped with the weight of his knee on the edge as he shifted over her. She must have come to some kind of peace about her adoption because there was no mistaking her intent focus on the moment. On him.

And he intended to work like hell to ensure she wouldn't be so quick to leave.

One button at a time he flicked open her blouse, exposing inch by tempting inch of creamy skin, see-through lace, more skin. After so long without her, he soaked up the sight of her, the curves of her breasts, the dip of her waist. In a double-edged torment he ruthlessly controlled the moment, drawing out her pleasure while sharpening his own to a painful edge.

He'd planned this afternoon on the private railcar to have her totally and completely to himself. No concerns about interruptions. Just Vanessa, with him, for hours on end. For once they didn't have an evening party to attend, so he'd arranged to have a limo pick them up at the train's after-dinner stop.

Meanwhile, he needed to use this time wisely, seductively. He thumbed along her rib cage, the fragile bones and translucent skin familiar under his fingers. Still he couldn't stop staring with appreciation, anticipation.

Her fingers worked down the fastenings on his shirt, mirroring his actions button for button until the cool conditioned air swept over his chest. She flattened her palms inside, branding him with her warm touch as she swept the crisp cotton away.

She raked her nails along his chest, lightly scoring. "This has been the longest two months of my life."

"I would have been happy to accommodate you at any time." He popped open her jeans and slid the zipper down, the rasp echoing the need grinding inside him. A low band of white lace peeked free, and he tucked his head to snap the elastic lightly with his teeth. "Thoughts of you, of this, have been killing me every second."

Nicolas inhaled, the erotic scent of her filling him. Throbbing, he nipped his way up her pale flat stomach, up to her breasts, her dusky nipples visible and taut and pushing against the peek-a-boo swirls of her lace bra. Her underwear was always white in her signature style, but in different patterns and cuts. Last summer he'd almost driven himself crazy watching her throughout the day, wondering what he would find once he undressed her.

Today, he knew. Lacey demi-bra and a thong. He took one hardened peak in his mouth, rolling it gently against his teeth, the dampened fabric a sweet abrasion against his tongue. She tasted like perfection.

Vanessa gasped, her blond hair tousled from his touch, one long strand pooling in the hollow of her throat. "How long does the train ride last? How far will we go?"

"As long—" he shifted his attention to her other breast "—and as far—" he tunneled his hand into the open vee of her jeans "—as you want."

"Don't make promises like that." She cupped his cheek and brought him up to her, face-to-face, her azure eyes stormy, intense. "We both know this ride has to end."

He couldn't miss her implied meaning about their future beyond this simple afternoon on the train. Of course nothing was ever simple with Vanessa, and he was quickly finding that intrigued him. If she wanted more, he would damn well provide.

Nuzzling into her silky hair, he peeled down her jeans while whispering in her ear, "Then we'll return again…and again…and again."

"I'm going to hold you to that promise."

His heartbeat pounded an extra thump in response.

She kicked her jeans off, her legs tangling with his, urging him to his side. She stayed with him until he rested on his back. He cupped her head, taking the kiss deeper, fuller. Her busy fingers roved, explored, disposed of his pants. And then he was in her hand.

His head pushed back into the pillows, his eyes closing as she stroked slowly, deliberately. A hitch in the train's motion provided tantalizing pleasure as they moved subtly against each other. He had to regain control fast or this would be over before they really got started.

Bracketing her waist with his hands, he lifted her as he sat up straighter on the bed. With a deft sweep of his hand, her bra came free, airborne as he tossed it away to land on the floor. She filled his hands, her breasts swelling into his palms with a sweet abundance his memory hadn't done justice. Her head lolled, her lashes sweeping closed.

Yes, he'd been right to find this time away, to dispense with their reservations as surely as their clothes. A quick twist and snap and he'd done away with her lacey thong, the final barrier between them. She straddled him as they sat face-to-face.

He looked his fill. Their time in the sauna had been fast and frenzied. This would be different.

Her silvery blond hair slithered over one shoulder, ends teasing along the tip of her breast. For a moment he noticed that she had the barest of tan lines—and then he could think of nothing but the slick press of her core against the throbbing length of him.

The chandelier swayed overhead with the gentle rocking of the railcar, shifting light and shadows over her skin like phantom fingers stroking her in all the places he ached to explore.

Fingertips to his cheek, she scratched lightly along the stubble he never seemed able to completely shave away. "I'm all for savoring the moment, Nicolas, but if you don't take me soon, the motion of this train is going to finish me."

She rolled her hips against him until the head of his arousal pressed closer. All he had to do was thrust and he would be inside her again. He clamped his jaw hard against the temptation to throw away caution again, and palmed the protection he'd tucked just under the rim of the tea set. Vanessa looked at the condom in his hand and frowned. Yeah, he understood her frustration—they'd come so close to forgetting about birth control altogether.

Frenetic need filled him now as it had that night in the sauna. He'd almost forgotten then, withdrawing just in time. He would do better by her this time. Vanessa stayed silent, chewing on her bottom lip while he sheathed himself.

Her hands on his shoulders, she lowered herself onto him and he clutched her hips as he wrestled with restraint—tough to do, given the soft feel of her flesh around him. Nicolas leaned back against the headboard as she hooked her legs around his waist, her arms around his neck.

Sighing, she teased his chest with her breasts, skimming kisses over his mouth. His tongue stroked in sync with his thrusts until he stopped thinking and just felt her around him. In his senses. It seemed right, given that he couldn't get her out of his thoughts even when they weren't together.

The humming vibration and swaying of the car intensified every movement she made, her sighs and moans of pleasure echoing in the dimly lit cabin. He rolled her onto her back, still intimately connected.

Vanessa's arms clutched him closer, her legs wrapping tighter until her heels dug into him. With each urgent rocking of her hips, she whispered her wants, and damn how he enjoyed the way she made it crystal clear what she needed and how she made her feel. Every sexy word and hitch in her breathing stoked him higher, harder, closer to the edge, but he wasn't going there alone. He thrust and waited, watching for the telltale flush spreading over Vanessa's creamy flesh. She arched and moaned, her fingernails biting into his back.

Finally, finally he could let go. Release jetted through him, intensified by her body gripping him in pulsing waves, drawing out the sensations until— He slumped to rest on his elbows before rolling beside her and gathering her perspiration-slicked body to his.

They must have drifted off because the next thing he knew, the sun was setting outside the window. He dragged the comforter from around their feet and draped it over them.

Stirring, Vanessa snuggled closer with a sigh and mumbled, "How late is it?"

"Almost supper time. The refrigerator is well-stocked. Would you like to take a look and decide what calls to your appetite?"

A sleepy smile dug dimples in her cheeks, still pink from stubble burn. "Surprise me. You've done well with that today."

He skimmed her shoulder with the back of his knuckles. "Spend the night with me. We can stay on the train. I can have the limo pick us up farther down the line."

Her smile faded and she fidgeted with the covers. "My father waits up. I know I'm an adult, but it seems cruel to worry him."

"What about telling him the truth?" The words were out before he thought about them, but once said... The secret meetings had been stimulating, and his conscience hadn't bothered him since they weren't sleeping together. But now? His principles demanded honesty. He would treat her and their relationship with respect. "A simple phone call, and your father will know we are a couple again."

She bolted upright, the comforter clasped to her chest, her hair tousled around her face in sexy disarray. "You're willing to take the scrutiny of dating me, of being connected to the Hughes family and the Bridgehampton Polo Club?"

Nicolas pushed to his feet to give himself distance from the distracting scent of their lovemaking, not because he was uncomfortable with her question, damn it. "People will gossip, but that should be of no concern to us."

He'd hesitated a second too long before answering her. He knew from the retreat in her eyes that she'd sensed his concern about possible bad PR and was upset by his gut reaction. Honor dictated he be upfront about their growing relationship, but that didn't mean he was comfortable with the decision. He had a professional reputation to maintain, something he thought Vanessa would understand better now than she had last year.

And what did she want? The flash of uncertainty in her eyes made him wonder if she wanted more than a last fling to get over each other.

Then she blinked, a smile curving her kissed-full lips. She wriggled to lean against the headboard, the rustle of sheets serenading him with promises.

To hell with food or phone calls. They still had hours left before they returned home.

The mattress gave beneath his knee as he returned to the bed. She opened her mouth and he kissed her before she could speak. Every word they'd spoken seemed to slide between them like layers of clothes, keeping them from the one way they communicated without confusion. Her fingers crawled up his chest and into his hair, urging him to stretch out beside her.

He understood her need to keep the affair private. Hell, he agreed. But he also knew he'd somehow fallen short in assuaging the concern that was evident in her eyes.

The next morning, Vanessa zipped up the side of her tennis skirt and stifled a yawn. She and Nicolas had made love until minutes before the train stopped. They'd tossed on their clothes and rushed to the waiting limo that had driven them home by midnight. She'd actually managed to tiptoe past her father's room with only a groggy "Night, Nessa" drifting out into the hall.

Still, the truth couldn't be avoided any longer. She would have to tell Nicolas about the baby, and soon. Her plan to wait until the end of the season was fatally flawed. She simply couldn't look into Nicolas's eyes while making love and keep such an important secret from him. How could she condemn her parents for concealing the truth, then turn around and do nearly the same thing to Nicolas? She refused to behave like a self-indulgent brat any longer.

Before she told him, she would need to prepare her father for the fallout. She had promised to meet Nicolas for lunch after a tennis game with her brother. She'd been surprised when her brother called to schedule the match. He was usually a workaholic, but he vowed he could step outside the polo club office for a quick game at the Seven Oaks courts.

After their tense summer, she was grateful he'd offered the olive branch. His surprise relationship with his assistant, Julia, seemed to be softening the harsher edge of her intensely ambitious brother.

That was how a relationship should be—two people bringing out the best in each other. While Nicolas challenged her and excited her, did she make him as happy? She tried to shrug aside the memory of the withdrawal in Nicolas's eyes when they'd discussed the possibility of going public. He might not want this kind of scrutiny, but she was certain he would stand by her during the pregnancy. Beyond that, she didn't know.

And her father?

As she slid on her tennis shoes, memories from her childhood streamed through her mind of her dignified mogul daddy waving two horse puppets around and putting on different voices. Her mother may not have been ideal, but her father had showered her with attention and affection. She had a fine parenting role model in him.

Shoelaces tied, she grabbed her racket and headed for the

hall. Her father's door was open wide and she could see he was awake in his sitting room with a breakfast tray. Wearing a paisley robe and matching pajamas, he sat in a wingback chair by the bay window, a cane propped against his knee.

A thousand words and explanations churned through her mind and she struggled for the right way to start the conversation.

She gripped the door frame to steady herself and blurted, "Why didn't you tell me I'm adopted?"

Hell.

That wasn't what she'd meant to say at all.

Except now that it was out there, she couldn't call the words back. She waited with nerves prancing in her stomach.

Christian stilled for just a moment, then placed his fork full of eggs back on the tray by the single rose. He carefully folded his hands under his chin, every movement slow and precise as if buying time to gather his thoughts. "How did you find out?"

Exhaling hard, she strode into the room and sat on the ottoman in front of him as she'd done a thousand times as a child, waiting for him to tell the next story. After a while, she'd started creating puppets for him, stretching her imagination to the limits to come up with whacky characters, delighted to find out how he would incorporate them.

Today, she needed something more than stories. She needed the truth. "Does it really matter how I know?"

"We'd always planned to tell you, but you had such a rough time of it during your teenage years." His eyes broadcast his apology and regret. "I was afraid of losing you altogether. Then your mother died…"

He cleared his throat, twisting his wedding band around his finger.

Understanding crept in even as she wished he'd made a

different choice. She rested her fingers over his bruised hand. "You've had a lot on your plate lately."

"I like to think I would have told you eventually, but I can't lie." He squeezed her fingers. "I honestly don't know."

It was not the answer she'd been hoping for, but at least they were talking openly. "Thank you for being honest about that."

He scrubbed a hand over his mouth. "I'm not a man who easily owns up to being wrong…"

His voice trailed off and he simply stared at her. She realized this was as close as her proud father could come to admitting he and her mother had screwed up. But she deserved to know more. She was no longer a child. And he could have died without ever revealing the truth.

What kind of hell would that have been for her if she'd found out afterward, never able to ask him about it face-to-face? Never been able to see the regret in his eyes that at least gave her some peace?

"Why did you adopt me? I would think after Sebastian, Mom would have realized motherhood wasn't her gig."

"Are you sure you're ready to hear everything?"

Her throat closed with nerves, but she wouldn't shy away—not when it counted. "I have to know."

"All right then," he said with a shaky breath. "One of my employees, a married man, had an affair with his secretary."

"She got pregnant?" She struggled not to press her hand to her stomach. While she couldn't imagine having an affair with a married man, she understood well the weight of secrets and fears for an unborn child. Vanessa pulled her concentration back to her father's words.

"They approached the company lawyer for help in arranging a private adoption for their baby. When your mother heard tests indicated the baby was a girl, she was insistent. We wanted to adopt the child, to adopt you."

"Because I was a girl?" Lynette had wanted a daughter? A bookend set of a son and daughter to round out the perfect family. Bitterness burned her mouth more fiercely than bile.

"She may not have been a warm, cookie-baking sort of mother, but she thought she was giving you everything by giving you what she wanted but never had growing up. I'm sorry she couldn't find it in herself to be a better mother to you and Sebastian."

She wanted to know more, to pry every bit of information out of him to better understand how her mother could have turned out so lacking in warmth or empathy. But the lines of exhaustion around her father's eyes stopped her.

Judging her mother wouldn't accomplish anything, wouldn't change the past. And wasn't she just as guilty in her own way of wounding other people because she hurt inside? She was trying to take steps toward being a better person, but she wasn't in any position to be sanctimonious.

Time to dig in and work if she wanted to be a better person.

A better mother.

She squeezed her father's hand again and started to stand. "Thank you for telling me."

"That's not everything."

Steeling herself for whatever he had to say, she sat again, determined to see this through even if it hurt.

"I went along with the adoption for your mother, but I hadn't counted on the way I would feel the first time I held my daughter." He leaned closer and cradled her face in his shaky hands. "You are my child, and my love for you isn't dependent on sharing the same DNA."

"I know," she said and realized she believed it without question. "Thank you for reminding me, though."

"We have to get everything right, Nessa, in case—"

"Stop." She clasped his wrists as if she could somehow root him in this life. "Please don't say it."

He reclined back in his chair, shaking his head sagely. "Not saying it doesn't make it any less real. Don't get me wrong, I'm thinking optimistically. I'm going to do whatever it takes to hang on. I've always wanted to bounce grandchildren on my knee."

Her breath caught in her throat.

Should she tell him about the baby? Would it be a comfort or a worry? She weighed the options. If he was nearing the end of his life… Vanessa swallowed hard.

She could tell him later, after she told Nicolas. Better to know where he stood before talking to her father. In an ideal world, she and Nicolas would tell him together.

"Daddy, I hope and pray you'll be around to applaud your grandchildren at their graduations, but if—" she gulped back tears that threatened to choke off words "—if that can't be, I promise I'll tell my children all the puppet stories you shared with me. And I'll teach them to stomp the hell out of those divots."

He smiled, big and broad, just the way she remembered from her childhood and in a way she hadn't seen the past year. Laughing, he held out his arms and she slid right into the familiar hug. His frame was surely slighter, but the hold was firm, steady. One she would feel lifting her up for the rest of her life.

She would need all that strength and more to put her heart on the line with Nicolas.

Five

"It was on the line!"

Standing beneath a striped awning outside the Seven Oaks gym, Nicolas heard Vanessa shout good-naturedly at her brother on the lush, green tennis court. The sound of her voice stirred memories of passionate hours spent on the train car together, stirring a need for more.

Sun already baking overhead even though the clock tower only said eleven, he slicked a hand over his hair, still wet from the shower he'd taken after his morning regimen with the team. The Seven Oaks Farm had top-of-the-line workout facilities as well as tennis courts…and, of course, a sauna.

Any more time spent thinking about the sauna and he would have to head to the gym shower again.

Stepping aside and nodding politely as Sheikh Adham left the building, Nicolas kept his eyes firmly locked on Vanessa arching back, tossing the ball in the air and swatting a clean serve. She swiped an arm over her forehead, shifting from foot to foot as she watched for her brother's return hit.

Yes, he could most definitely stand here and take in the view of Vanessa in her short white tennis skirt. All the other people by the pool might as well have faded away.

Vanessa and her brother lobbed and volleyed teasing comments back and forth with each sweep of the yellow ball over the net. There was no mistaking the bond of affection between them. Hughes would be pissed to find out about the secret affair—not that his sister's love life should be any of his business. But Nicolas didn't like the notion that he would cause trouble between the siblings.

In fact, he didn't much like the notion of sneaking around, either. He couldn't deny the growing realization that he wanted more with Vanessa, beyond the polo season, and that meant coming out with their relationship.

Once he had Vanessa alone—he'd arranged a private dinner at a local French restaurant—he would discuss the proper time and manner to reveal their relationship to her family. And to the press. Decision made, he started to leave. Better to let her enjoy her game with her brother. If Hughes caught him watching Vanessa, Nicolas wasn't so sure he could keep his face impassive.

Vanessa stumbled, missing the ball. Nicolas hesitated. She regained her footing and he exhaled. Hard. Damn, he never would have thought a time would come when he would wear his heart on his sleeve. He definitely needed to regain his own footing before he had the discussion with Vanessa.

Pivoting, he started back into the gym.

"Vanessa!"

Hughes's shouted call carried an urgency that made Nicolas freeze in his tracks. He turned, just in time to see Vanessa crumple to the ground unconscious.

Nicolas had considered himself fearless. Until now.

Seeing Vanessa sprawled on the ground, passed out on the court, dumped fear into his gut. To hell with waiting for the right time to reveal his feelings for Vanessa. He didn't care who saw how he felt about her.

Nicolas tossed aside his gym bag and sprinted toward Vanessa.

Vanessa pushed through the foggy layers of unconsciousness.

Had she overslept? Disorientation muddled her mind. She sank deeper into the cushiony surface beneath her. Voices swirled—in her dreams?

"What the hell are you doing here?" her brother demanded.

"Hughes, this is not the time or place," Nicolas answered, his voice worried.

The baby. Their baby. Oh, God.

Vanessa clamped a hand to her stomach and pried her eyes open. She felt fine, other than dizzy, but still, fear swept over her.

She blinked fast and saw Nicolas and Sebastian standing nose to nose a few feet away. A quick look around told her they were in Sebastian's office at the polo club's headquarters—her father's old office. Someone must have carried her to the large leather sofa. How long had she been out?

A cool hand touched her brow, and she found Sebastian's fiancée, Julia, kneeling beside her. Brass sconces illuminated the concern on her future sister-in-law's face.

"Julia?"

"You fainted. Have you checked your levels recently? Where's your meter so we can check now?"

"Fainted?" Because of the baby or low blood sugar? "My meter is in my purse back in the locker room."

Nicolas and Sebastian went silent, then bolted across the room toward her. Nicolas beat him by a step.

"Vanessa?" He stroked back her hair as she struggled to sit up. "Are you all right?"

His own damp hair was slicked back. Wearing black slacks and a gray polo, he must have just completed his morning workout. She should have considered that when agreeing to meet her brother here, but who could have foreseen this?

She touched Nicolas's chest lightly. "I'm fine. Just a little woozy. A quick check of my blood sugar levels and there will be nothing to worry about."

He clasped her hand in his.

Sebastian growled protectively.

Nicolas scowled, his dark Latin eyes turning even darker.

"Gentlemen," Julia said with calm command as she stepped in front of Nicolas, tucking a tapestry pillow behind Vanessa, "why don't you both help by stepping outside. One of you can go look for her purse. The other can see if the paramedics have arrived. Make sure they know about Vanessa's diabetes."

Both men eyed each other warily, then made tracks toward the door.

"Thank you." Vanessa reclined back on the pillow, her head still woozy. "I don't think I could have handled them arguing right now."

"Just lie still. The paramedics are on their way." Julia tucked another pillow under Vanessa's feet. "I can't believe we don't have a doctor playing tennis here this morning."

Vanessa tried to laugh at the joke, but fears for her baby overwhelmed her. "Julia? I need to talk to you. If I pass out again, be sure the paramedics know—"

"About your diabetes. Of course, I will," Julia reassured her.

"Not just that," Vanessa rushed to explain. This wasn't the

way she'd wanted the news to come out, but she didn't have the luxury of waiting. "Don't let them give me any drugs. Nobody knows yet, but, um, I'm pregnant—"

The echo of heavy footsteps stopped her short. Had the paramedics arrived already? She wasn't sure how long she'd been out.

Framed in the doorway stood her brother and Nicolas. The room swirled again, and this time it had nothing to do with blood-sugar levels or pregnancy. The stunned—then thunderous—looks on both men's faces left her with no doubts. They'd heard her revelation. Her secrets were out. Sebastian knew about her relationship with Nicolas.

And Nicolas knew about their baby.

Waiting outside the E.R. exam room, Nicolas struggled to keep his emotions in check.

He was known for his calm under any circumstances. But today had blown that out of the water. He was furious, wrecked, leveled by Vanessa's revelation at the polo club. She was pregnant with his child. And yes, he knew it was his. He could read that in her expression clearly enough when her eyes had met his.

Thank God he'd kept his mouth shut then, because he wasn't sure what would have come out once he learned she'd been lying to him for weeks. Nothing had changed. She was still keeping secrets—and may have endangered his child.

She was still the same immature woman. He'd been a wishful fool to think otherwise, simply because he'd needed to justify climbing back into bed with her.

Nicolas paced, shoes squeaking on industrial tile. He wanted to punch something.

At least Hughes and his fiancée were staying quiet. He and Vanessa's brother seemed to have reached an unspoken understanding that there would be no confrontation right now. Not that Hughes's fiancée would have let them exchange words. The woman was a velvet-gloved, stern taskmaster.

She was right. Vanessa's health was paramount. He was angry, without question, but he would hold himself in check.

And he wasn't leaving Vanessa's side.

At least her baby was okay—even if her relationship with Nicolas appeared uncertain.

Unable to get Nicolas's thunderous expression out of her mind, Vanessa finished dressing in the E.R. exam room. The paramedics had transported her to the hospital, a frightening five-minute ride. Her physician had met her at the hospital and checked her over. The doctor had reassured her that the fainting spell was not related to her diabetes and that everything appeared fine with the baby. Passing out had simply been a byproduct of pregnancy. He'd prescribed a lazy afternoon in bed and given her his pager number if she had any concerns.

She still had plenty of concerns. First of all, she needed to read a whole lot more about becoming a mother, because she did not want to screw this up. And if she was overdoing it, by God, she would make an art form of settling down.

Then there were other concerns, the ones centered on the baby's father. The sterile air stung her nose as she sniffed back tears. Nicolas had come to mean so much to her this summer, even more than she'd expected after a year of thinking about him, of missing him. Seeing that look of betrayal on his face had hurt so much—she wasn't sure how to begin making it right.

Vanessa stepped out of the exam room and found Nicolas right outside the door, leaning against the wall, waiting. Alone.

"Where's Sebastian?" she asked nervously.

"Julia persuaded him to leave once the doctor assured us all was well with you. Your brother put up a fight, but she convinced him that was the very reason he should leave. You need peace, not controversy." He touched her back. "I have arranged for a car to drive us."

She tried to get a read off his face, but her intense lover, the charmer of the past two months, had disappeared. The old Nicolas was back, the man in complete control of his emotions. She sure could use some tenderness. Maybe he was just waiting until they were alone. After all, they still hadn't officially come out about their relationship.

The sun blinded her momentarily, her eyes adjusting as a limo pulled up alongside her.

Nicolas slid his arm around her waist, steadying her, not letting go until she was safely inside. His care touched her ragged nerves as firmly as his hand held her body. He settled her into the backseat then sat across from her.

Across?

So much for warm fuzzies. She wished she could sink into his arms and rest her head on his broad chest while he reassured her he was excited about the baby.

After giving the driver her father's address, Nicolas folded his arms over his chest and watched her with the detached air of a physician observing his patient.

The limo glided out of the parking lot and onto the main road. The drive would be short back to her father's house. Even though every instinct inside her shouted to wait, to talk to him later when they were both calmer, she couldn't stop the words from tumbling out of her mouth.

She resisted the urge to grab him by his collar and shake him. Instead, she folded her hands carefully in her lap and wished she had on something a little more substantial than a tennis skirt. "Aren't you going to ask about the pregnancy? I know you overheard me tell Julia."

His jaw flexed, all his muscles visibly tensed even though he sat stone still. "All the more reason not to discuss this now. You need to rest and take care of yourself."

"Don't you think I understand that?" She pulled in the rising hysteria that grew with every second he stayed in that seat across from her. She needed to hear how he felt, damn it. "I went to my doctor right after I took a home pregnancy test. He's already referred me to a high-risk OB because of my diabetes. I understand the risks and I know how to be careful."

"You're keeping the baby then."

"Yes, I am." Certainty settled within her for the first time. She was her own person, in her own situation. "I want our child regardless of whether or not you're in my life."

"Our child," he said slowly.

She realized that until that moment, she hadn't officially confirmed that the baby was his.

No wonder he'd been distant. She leaned forward and rested a tentative hand on his knee. "Nicolas, this is your baby. I got pregnant that evening when we made love in the sauna."

"But you weren't going to tell me." A tic twitched in the corner of his eye.

Of course he was angry over being kept in the dark—but not necessarily because of the baby. Relief swamped her. "I was waiting until after the season."

"Why would that make any difference?"

His cold voice iced her relief. She pulled her hand back. "I didn't want to upset my father."

"What does that have to do with telling me? I can see waiting until after the season before telling him, but I have a right to know."

She couldn't argue with his logic, since she'd come to the same conclusion herself. "I had changed my mind about waiting and was going to tell you tonight."

"So you say."

Shock and anger rooted her to the seat. "You think I'm lying?"

He shook his head, going silent again.

She smacked the leather seat with her hands. "Talk to me, damn it. You're upsetting me far more by keeping your thoughts to yourself."

"I just think it all sounds convenient. Nothing's changed from last year."

The reminder of his recurring accusations about her immaturity drained the blood from her face. "That's not fair."

He looked out the window.

"Don't you dare clam up on me now!"

"You're being too emotional," he answered in the same low voice he used to calm his horses. "It's not good for you or the baby."

She was not an overworked pony! She was a woman with her heart on the line. "Of course I'm emotional. You're dumping me again."

"Now is not the time," he said, still using that cool voice as the limo pulled up outside her family home. "Perhaps you are right. We should wait to discuss this at the end of the season."

"You don't want your baby?"

His eyes went darker with emotion. "Make no mistake, I will be a part of our child's life."

But he said nothing about her, and she couldn't overlook that omission.

She bolted from the car and sprinted up the steps toward the double doors, brass knobs gleaming, welcoming her into the haven of home.

She'd been a fool all summer long, a fool to think she could make a game of her relationship with Nicolas, that somehow she could minimize the power of her feelings. Throwing him out of her life last year had been painful, but it was nothing compared with the ache twisting her heart now. She loved Nicolas Valera, a man who didn't trust or respect her.

A man who didn't love her back.

Six

He'd screwed up, big-time.

Nicolas shouldered through the scores of spectators gathered for the afternoon game. His team wasn't playing, but he needed to analyze the other ponies in action for future matchups.

Instead, he could only think of finding Vanessa.

She'd ignored his calls the night before and this morning. He wanted to apologize for not supporting her at a time when they should be banding together. God, how he regretted hurting her feelings with his insensitive behavior.

And if she wouldn't accept his apology? Then they at least needed to get on a more civil footing and make plans before the pregnancy became public knowledge. So far not even a whisper had leaked, but they couldn't count on that lasting much longer.

Sweat beaded along his back, the full force of the afternoon sun intact for at least another hour until it dipped below the tree line at the western edge of the field. Weaving around three men setting up a tailgate party on the lush green lawn, he searched—and still no Vanessa.

He wasn't accustomed to losing control. His sisters had a more stereotypical Latin temper, but Nicolas had always prided himself on his cool calm. Until he'd met Vanessa.

The woman tapped into emotions he'd never felt, good and bad. While wrestling with his anger, determined to keep things low-key for both her well-being and their baby's, he'd lost sight of how much she would need his reassurance.

She was carrying his child, a fact that still shook the ground beneath his feet. His brain filled with images of a little girl with Vanessa's face and his hair, tiny feet stamping divots and taking the world by storm.

He felt eyes on him and pivoted...only to find a pair of women in nearly identical sundresses and sandals staring, then waving and giggling. Groupies. He wasn't interested.

Finally, he spotted a familiar face. Down the sidelines, he saw Vanessa's father, Christian Hughes, in a wheelchair. The ailing man had lost at least twenty or thirty pounds since last season, but he still had a commanding gestalt that couldn't be missed. He may have made a concession to his illness with the wheelchair, but there was no sickroom blanket resting over his knees. The older man wore neatly pressed tan slacks with a polo shirt under a linen sports coat and a perfectly folded kerchief peeking out of the pocket.

A plaid driving hat protected his shaved head from the sun. And behind the chair, no nurse. Nicolas slowed his step. Sebastian Hughes stood watch behind his father.

How much had he told his dad about Vanessa and the baby? Time to find out.

Nicolas charged forward. Christian Hughes eyed him impassively, giving nothing away.

"Good afternoon, sir," Nicolas said carefully.

"Valera," Christian nodded, "always nice to see the players out mingling with the crowd. Good for the draw."

Sebastian silently assessed him with cool eyes.

"Actually, Mr. Hughes, I'm looking for Vanessa."

A spark of surprise glinted in the older man's eyes for an instant. Nicolas glanced up at Sebastian, who shook his head. Vanessa's father didn't know. Interesting.

He held on to his hope that he could stand by Vanessa's side when she told Christian Hughes. He wanted to be there for support, and to reassure her father he cared for Vanessa and the baby. He would be there for both of them.

Christian raised a frail but steady hand and gestured left. "She's about five tents down, away from the field. Look for the red-and-white-striped tent with all the children."

He couldn't have heard right. "Pardon me? Where did you say?"

"The red-and-white tent, the child care area. She's arranged activities for children during matches." He smiled proudly. "I believe it's story hour right now. She makes a point of dropping in then."

His perception of her shifted and settled as he heard of the considerate way she'd seen to the needs of others, from the spectators to their restless children. How could he have not known that about her? Now that he thought about it, this certainly fit with the impressions he'd gleaned this summer of added maturity, of a deeper sensitivity for the needs of those around her. She'd certainly been there for her father.

He could picture her with kids. He'd bet anything her impulsiveness and quick laugh—and the mischievous gleam in her blue eyes—would attract children by the dozen.

"Thank you, Mr. Hughes." *For the directions and the additional insight.*

He sidestepped the chair. A lowly spoken "good luck" drifted on the wind from her brother as Nicolas covered grassy ground quickly on his way toward the red-and-white-striped tent. Had he heard that right? Then again, maybe Sebastian wasn't rooting for him as much warning him. No doubt Vanessa was not pleased with him.

Shouldering past a pair of Shetland ponies set up for children to ride, he heard Vanessa's voice above the hubbub of activity. Her warm, inviting tone drew his feet forward even faster.

Then her voice changed. She lowered it as if imitating another person. Stopping at a large metal pole at the back of the tent, Nicolas peered into the shaded depths.

Vanessa came into focus.

Her sunglasses were off, her eyes bright and completely unguarded. A half dozen kids sat cross-legged around her while adults wearing Bridgehampton Polo Club uniforms stood along the periphery. He looked closer, frowning. Yes, Vanessa wore finger puppets.

A smile tugging his mouth, he leaned against the metal pole and listened. She gestured with a fairy princess on her pinky and then introduced the horse on her thumb with a mane made of fuzzy black yarn. She wove tales of a magical polo-pony adventure, featuring "Nessa" and "Nicky." Vanessa was so absorbed in her storytelling, she didn't even notice his arrival. At different points in the tale, she swapped out tiny puppets for other supporting characters hidden away in her huge purse, yet Nessa and Nicky stayed in place throughout. He wasn't so sure he liked being referred to as Nicky, but he appreciated being in her imagination because, God knows, she was featured in his every thought.

But it was more than the puppet tale that tugged him as he stood there. It was the space she'd converted into a child's haven that drove home that a sweet, dedicated and caring woman lived beneath her beautiful exterior.

She'd done more than blow up a few balloons and hire a

clown. The play area had backdrops that had been painted in rainbow colors with the carefree enthusiasm a child might use on an easel drawing. Various stations were set up in the corners—arts and crafts, snacks, even a few cots for tired tots. An inflatable slide hummed with air off to the side. A miniature basketball court awaited a game.

And at the center of it all was a woman he'd misjudged. A woman who guarded herself so carefully he hadn't seen the transformation she'd undergone, which was as vast as the changes she'd made to the red-and-white-striped tent.

His eyes and ears told him what he should have realized long ago. The Vanessa he'd gotten to know this summer was the real woman, a woman he would have understood better last year had he focused on more than getting her naked at every opportunity. He'd almost missed the boat again by failing to come through for her yesterday the way he should have. The truth stared him in the face as clearly as those finger puppets waving through the air.

And today, he intended to make sure Vanessa and the entire Bridgehampton community knew just how much he loved her.

Her heart still aching, Vanessa stood on the sidelines of the polo match, grateful for the sunglasses shading her tear-stained eyes. She forced herself to sample the luncheon buffet set up beside her under a tent, but the catered fare tasted like dust.

After story time with the children, she hadn't been able to hold back her sobs any longer. She'd cried her heart out in a bathroom stall—hurt, mad and downright lost. How could she make her world right again?

Watching the match now was pure torture, and Nicolas wasn't even playing today. How much worse would it be when she had to see him and know she couldn't have him?

Everyone else around her was abuzz with excitement over being at the epicenter of the Hamptons' social scene. The Bridgehampton Polo Club events had become Long Island's playground. The outrageously good-looking players were the main attraction, of course. As a teenager, she'd fantasized about scores of them. Now, her thoughts centered on only one.

The one she couldn't have.

She wanted to find her old spunk and fight for him, but she wasn't even sure where to begin. She couldn't afford to risk upheaval and discord when they needed to communicate peacefully for their baby's sake.

The halftime horn blew, jolting her from her thoughts.

Out of habit, she slid her purse from her shoulder and dug for her shoes. As she swapped out her heels, she found she simply didn't have the urge to stomp anything. She wanted to go back to that stall and cry some more.

This was so unlike her, and yet she couldn't bring herself to blame it on pregnancy hormones. For the first time in her life, she had no idea what to do. She'd always fought for what she wanted, but Nicolas had made it clear he didn't want scenes.

He didn't want *her*.

A hum started in the crowd. Vanessa looked over her shoulder to see what had caused the ruckus. She saw nothing, except a bunch of faces looking past her.

She followed the direction of their gazes. A horse galloped along the sidelines, a sorrel pony with a coat as shiny as a new penny. She knew the horse well, and the man astride Maximo. Confusion knitted her brows together. Nicolas wasn't playing today—it wasn't his match, after all—so why was he here? And why was he riding directly toward her?

Her heart flip-flopped in her chest. He pulled up on the reins, the horse stopping just an arm's reach away from her. An expectant hush settled over the throng gathering tighter and tighter around them. Maximo, unflappable as always, stayed still as stone. Nicolas's face, however, was full of emotion, his impassive look long gone. Heart in her throat, hopefulness fluttered to life inside her.

His shoulders back, head regally high, he winked at her before shifting his attention to the crowd. "Is there a reporter out there anywhere?"

Bodies jostled before no fewer than seven microphones poked through the crowd toward Nicolas.

What was he doing? Nicolas had never courted the media outside his carefully chosen endorsement spots. And heaven knew, he'd never wanted to share the spotlight with her. Hope fluttered faster.

"I have an announcement," Nicolas broadcast, his sexy accent rippling along the light summer breeze. "Last year I made a terrible mistake in letting a special lady slip away, a mistake I do not intend to repeat. I want to make sure the world knows I am in love with Vanessa Hughes. And whether or not she will have me, I want everyone to realize how much I admire this amazing woman."

Her knees turned as soft as the rice pudding she'd served the kids after lunch.

Dreamy sighs echoed through the crowd, but nothing was louder than the pounding of her heart, the gasp in her throat. Because Nicolas was here, in front of all of Bridgehampton, making a wonderfully uncharacteristic scene on her behalf, laying his heart on the line for her.

Flashes went off. Shutters clicked. Whistles and applause stirred the crowd. Happy tears fell unchecked down her cheeks.

He raised his hand for silence before continuing, "I have plenty more I could say about Vanessa, but it is best I save it for her ears only, you understand." He dismounted, his eyes meeting and holding hers for the first time. He extended his hand. "Would you please do me the honor of joining me for a ride?"

If she went with him on the horse, she would be deciding her whole future right now, embracing a lifetime with this passionate man who could hide his true feelings so well. Or… she could simply walk away.

The decision was easy. Hadn't she just experienced a small taste of how much it hurt to be without him? She trusted him. She loved him. They would figure out the rest together.

With a chorus of songbirds singing in crescendo, Vanessa placed her hand in his, happily sealing her fate.

The crowd roared their approval. With a strong but gentle touch, Nicolas lifted her onto Maximo before settling behind her. His arms bracketed her as he held the reins. A light click and Maximo trotted forward. Nicolas's chest offered an amazing place to rest her head, his signature scent swirling around her along with cheers and applause from the throng.

Vanessa caught a quick glimpse of her father and brother. Her dad lifted his hands, clapping. Even Sebastian shot them a thumbs-up. Peace settled inside her as she soaked in the support from her family. Any concerns or aches over the adoption scattered faster than chunks of turfs from under Maximo's hooves.

She tipped her face up to Nicolas, nuzzling his neck as he navigated his way out of the crowd. "I don't know what made you change your mind about us, but you'd better find a place for us to be alone, or I'm going to cause another scandal."

"As long as you're creating that scandal with me, count me in." His brown eyes glinted with amusement, arousal, love.

He swept her sunglasses up onto her head, the bright sun glinting off of the barn roof in the distance. Then she couldn't see at all as her eyes closed for his kiss. Her world narrowed to just the two of them, the taste of him on her lips, the bristle of his cheek against her skin, the sensuous way he dipped his nose toward her hair and inhaled.

Nicolas secured her against his chest with an arm and urged Maximo into a canter toward the pear orchard near the fields. Her heart pounded in time with horse's hooves. They slowed to a stop in the same clearing where they'd tucked away for a clandestine moment during a party. Now, glossy white ribbons and bows were draped from the branches.

"Oh, Nicolas," she gasped. "How did you manage all of this?"

"Bridgehampton Polo Club hires only the best staff."

Her laughter bubbled up and over like champagne freed from the bottle. "Of course. I should have known."

He slid from the horse and raised his hands to help her dismount with reverent tenderness. Then he knelt in front of her. She tugged his arm.

"Really, you don't have to do this. No one is looking now," she grinned.

His face went as solemn as she'd ever seen it.

"You're looking, and that is what matters most to me." He clasped her fingers. "Vanessa, will you do me the honor of becoming my wife?"

In spite of the sincerity and emotion she saw in his eyes, a final doubt lingered. "If you're saying this because of the baby—"

He squeezed her hand lightly to silence her. "I am asking because I love you. You already know how much I want you. But I also love you—the way you stand up for yourself, the way you care for your father, the way your eyes dance as you share finger puppet stories."

"How did you find out about the puppet play?" she asked, incredulous.

He traced her lips, caressing. "Does that matter? All that

matters to me right now is that you give me a lifetime to prove how happy we can be together."

Then her mind zeroed in on the most important part of his declaration. "You love me?"

"Completely. And I intend to make sure you never have to phrase that as a question again." His bold face furrowed with regret over the hurt he'd caused.

How easy it was to forgive him when he'd found such a dramatic way of making amends.

He continued. "I think we bring balance to each other, in addition to the love and passion. Together, we have everything."

The peace in his eyes matched the quiet joy in her heart. Her last reservation was put to rest.

"Yes." She knelt into his arms. "Yes, yes and again yes, I love you and want to be your wife."

Pulling her close, he kissed her firmly, shuddering with unmistakable relief. This unshakable man, her cool, collected lover, had been afraid she would say no? Tears of happiness stung her eyes. She pressed her face to the warmth of his neck, savoring the fact that she would have years to enjoy his embrace endlessly.

He nuzzled her hair. "So how does the story of Nessa and Nicky end? I had to leave before you finished."

Smiling, she looked up at him. "They worked together and won the match, of course."

"Hmmm…" He rested his forehead against hers. "I am sorry I didn't come through for you right away."

"We're here now."

She stayed in his arms and the moment until Maximo pawed the ground impatiently.

Nicolas glanced at his horse. "Thank you for reminding me, my friend." He looked back at Vanessa, a heated gleam in his eyes as he stood. "I have more planned for you today."

"More? But I already have everything I want right in front of me.

"I can think of one more thing that I want."

"What would that be?" She would do her best to deliver.

"I want to see an engagement ring on your finger by sunset. What do you say to a shopping expedition before dinner?"

Certainly filled her heart as surely happy tears filled her eyes. "I say absolutely yes."

He reached for her, his hand steady and sure, his thoughtfully romantic ribbons and bows rustling overhead like a sentimental bridal bower. Anticipation tingling through her, she clasped his hand and settled atop Maximo with him.

Nicolas brushed her ear with a kiss. "Don't you want to know where we're going after we pick out the ring?"

"Surprise me."

And she knew without a doubt this intensely driven, sexy man would always deliver a winner.

* * * * *

HIS ACCIDENTAL FIANCÉE

EMILY McKAY

To the fabulous women (and men) of ARWA,
the best RWA chapter in the world.
Y'all are wonderful, supportive and just dang fun.

One

Connor Stone looked up from his drink and saw the next woman he was going to take to bed.

He knew it the instant he saw her standing by the bar in Riffs, the jazz bar where he was sipping away his Thursday night. The fact that she was there with a date didn't particularly worry him.

He had met his buddy Tim for drinks. Connor had been watching the gorgeous blonde since she'd arrived ten minutes earlier. Based on the way the guy was acting, they were probably on a bad blind date. He kept glancing at his watch and tugging at his tie.

Though why a guy would try to ditch a woman like her, Connor couldn't guess. Her face had an extravagant beauty that made her impossible to ignore. Her movements had a grace and sensuality to them, as if she moved in rhythm to the quartet playing standards in the corner. Through the constantly moving crowd, he could see her well enough to tell her body was made for sin. Unfortunately, all those lush curves were encased in a demure navy dress. Why would a woman with a body like that shield herself in a layer of protective armor meant to hide her most appealing attributes?

Connor was debating whether to wait for her date to leave before approaching her when Tim nudged him. "If you're thinking about hitting on her, I should warn you, you're going to strike out."

Something about Tim's tone irritated him. Tim was a work friend, and frankly, Connor had always thought Tim got by on family connections rather than hard work.

"Don't tell me you know her."

Tim smiled smugly, then leaned closer to be heard over the music. "Brittney Hannon. Daughter of Senator Jonathon P. Hannon. Just last week, *New York Personality* magazine did a big interview with her. Called her 'The Last Good Girl in America'."

Connor eyed his target. She did have a certain puritanical quality to her. She wore her blond hair long and straight. If Marcia Brady had come to the bar directly from Sunday school, this is what she'd look like.

He'd always had a thing for Marcia Brady.

"You think good girls can't be tempted?"

As he asked the question, Brittney looked up from her nervous date and met Connor's gaze. The awareness between them arced across the room. He felt it like a strong kick to the gut.

"I'll bet you a thousand dollars you can't get her into bed by the end of the summer," Tim said.

Brittney looked down at her drink, clearly disconcerted. Connor smiled. "I'll have her in my bed by the end of the week."

Tim just laughed. "You're going to have to work fast then. From what I've heard, she's a polo fan."

"So?"

"Boy, you really don't follow society news, do you?" Tim looked at him like he was a moron.

"I follow the financial news."

"Well, she'll be in Bridgehampton all summer for the polo season. While you're in town, working." Tim gave him a punch in the arm. "You should get your head out from under that rock and play a little."

Easy for Tim to say. His family was old money. All Tim had to do was sit back and make sure he didn't screw up too badly.

Connor, on the other hand, came from a blue-collar family in Pennsylvania. If he didn't work his ass off, his clients lost millions. And if that happened, his career as a hedge-fund manager would be over. "I gotta work hard so I can play hard," he explained.

But the truth was, he *had* been working too hard lately. It was time to cut loose. And Brittney Hannon was just the woman to do it with. As if on cue, her nervous date tossed down a few bills, gestured toward the door and made a run for it.

The guy was clearly an idiot, but at least he hadn't stiffed Brittney with the bill. But his loss was Connor's gain.

This is going to be too easy.

Being dubbed "The Last Good Girl in America" was killing Brittney Hannon's love life.

She sighed as her date abandoned her at Riffs. If her drink hadn't *just* arrived, she'd leave too. But she figured she'd earned the appletini.

In the two weeks since the profile had run in *New York Personality*, she'd had no fewer than three disastrous dates.

She blamed the article. She'd agreed to the interview as a favor to her college sorority sister, Margot. It was supposed to be an in-depth look at how Brittney was using her Web design background to manage her father's "cyber campaign." Instead, Margot had taken a few quotes from the actual interview and cobbled them together with bits and pieces of private conversations from over the past decade. The resulting "profile" made Brittney out to be a sanctimonious prude who was on the hunt for a husband and who encouraged women to withhold sex in exchange for an engagement ring. There was nothing overtly libelous about the article, but the title had not been meant as a compliment.

And this was exactly why she didn't talk to the press very often. She was too blunt. Too outspoken. Too honest. And it always got her in trouble. Which was why she hadn't confronted Margot after reading the profile. Why risk giving the woman more fuel? She had decided long ago she was better off giving reporters nothing interesting to say about her.

For now, her love life was taking a hit. The best she could figure, most men simply weren't interested in working any harder than they had to. They saw her as a pain, rather than interesting challenge. She was trying to view this as simply a way to weed out the men who scared easily. But it wasn't much consolation. She'd just have to suffer through it. It wouldn't kill her.

The truth was, she was more concerned about how the profile would affect her father's campaign. Zoe, her father's senior aide, had assured her the profile wasn't as bad as she thought. And then politely reminded her to schedule any dealings with the press through the senator's office. Most of the time, Brittney's own views came off as too socially conservative for her father's urban constituents, and she had no talent for tempering her opinions to make them more palatable. In short, she was a total failure as a politician's daughter. As if it wasn't bad enough that the circumstances of her birth had cast suspicions on her father's morals.

She'd grown up knowing that marriage to her showgirl mother had nearly destroyed her father's budding career. That, combined with the fact that she was the very image of her mother, motivated her to stay out of trouble. She certainly didn't want to do any more damage to her father's career. Her mother might not be around anymore to create scandalous headlines, but Brittney certainly didn't want to remind anyone of her. She'd learned long ago, her safest course of action was to smile serenely, pose for the photos and keep her mouth shut.

And then Margot had come along asking for an interview. Brittney hadn't imagined that an innocent profile of her work on her father's campaign could cause any problems. But once again, her honesty had come back to bite her on the ass.

Thank goodness the polo season was just around the corner. The rich, famous and dissolute would descend on the Hamptons. They'd stir up enough gossip to satisfy even the most inquiring of minds. Within a week or two, everyone would forget about the silly profile. Then Brittney could enjoy the rest of the summer at her father's place on Long Pond. The house was secluded enough that she could get plenty of work done during the week, but close enough to Bridgehampton she could enjoy the social scene on the weekends.

In a discreet, quiet fashion.

No more interviews for her. For the rest of the summer, she was going to focus on keeping her nose clean and her mouth shut. Maybe by fall she would find a man brave enough to date her.

Normally, she wasn't much of a drinker, but since her date had abandoned her, she raised her martini, gave a silent toast to the door through which he'd left, and then downed the rest of it.

When she lowered the glass, her gaze met a pair of piercing blue eyes from across the room. The same man she'd seen earlier was still watching her. She tore her gaze away, but then a second later, looked back. Still there.

That piercing gaze of his was just the tip of the iceberg. He had jet-black hair, disheveled in a way that could be bought only from a very expensive hairdresser. His shoulders were broad and encased in Armani. The intensity of his eyes was balanced out by a rakish smile, full of charm and humor. Dimples slashed his cheeks, making it almost impossible to resist returning his smile. The overall combination resulted in a 'berg big enough to sink the most titanic of female hearts.

Everything about the man exuded sensual promise. The scary thing was, just once she wished she were the kind of woman who would take him up on it.

But no, she was Brittney Hannon, daughter of a prominent senator. Stalwart defender and representative of middle America's values. She truly was the last good girl in America. Unfortunately.

She set down her empty glass and picked up her clutch, ready to leave. When she looked up, he was there, standing beside the chair across from her.

"Mind if I join you?"

She should tell him that she did mind. Or better yet, that she was just leaving. She *knew* that. Instead, she nodded, allowing her purse to slip through her fingers and land back in her lap.

He gestured to a passing waitress to bring her another drink. "A woman as beautiful as you shouldn't be sitting in a bar alone."

Somehow, she'd expected better from him. "Do pickup lines that cheesy ever work for you?"

He smiled ruefully. "Only when I really mean them."

She wanted to resist but couldn't help smiling back. "Nice save."

The waitress brought her drink over. Brittney blinked in surprise at the bright green concoction. "I had to wait twenty minutes for my first drink to get here." She took a sip. "Do you have a name?"

She looked up at him. The heat from the intensity of his blue gaze burned through her, hotter than the warmth from the vodka in her drink.

The connection she felt almost made her sorry she'd looked into his eyes. It wasn't just that he was handsome and charming—she encountered handsome, charming men every day. No, there was something else about him. When he looked at her, she felt enticing. As if she were the only woman in the room. As if she were a sex goddess. And for a second there, she'd wanted to be that person for him. She wanted to be sexy and alluring.

"Connor Stone," he said.

She blinked. She'd nearly forgotten the question she'd asked. He was watching her, waiting for her to tell him her name. For a second she hesitated. Normally, she was proud of who she was, proud of being good. So what was it about this man that made her want to forget all of that, just for one night?

She took another generous sip of her drink. "I'm Brittney."

He raised his eyebrows. "Just Brittney?"

"Just Brittney."

He leveled that shrewd, assessing gaze at her, and she could have sworn he saw right through her. To the lies she was telling herself even now.

"Like Britney Spears," he supplied.

And just like that, who she really was came crashing back.

"No," she shook her head. "Not like Spears. More like the spaniel."

He chuckled at her self-deprecating analogy. The sound was low and sexy. It made her want to keep saying funny things so she could hear it again, but she was all out of witty repartee.

Her sorority sisters—Margot included—had come up with that assessment of her personality. Brittney...not like Spears, like the spaniel. Steadfast. Loyal. Dependable. And even if she wanted to be more like Spears for one night—reckless, careless and fun—she wasn't that person.

She set down the appletini and leaned forward. "I have to be honest. I'm not really this kind of woman."

"What kind of woman?"

"The kind who lets a stranger pick her up in a bar for a one-night stand."

He smiled a knowing smile. "I didn't really think you were."

"So I should go. Give you a chance to try with someone else." She nodded toward the room in general, where there were countless other women who'd cheerfully fill her empty chair.

Now he leaned forward. His gaze shifted from amused to something more intense. "Then I should be honest, too. That guy that you think I am—the one who'll hit on one woman, strike out and then mindlessly move on to the next—I'm not that kind of guy."

Surprised, she asked, "Then what kind of guy are you?"

"I'm the kind of guy who gets what I want."

Her throat tightened even as warmth spread through her limbs. It was an odd combination of dread and excitement. To cover her discomfort, she stood up. "Well, then, Connor Stone, you should prepare yourself to be disappointed."

He stood as well, extending his hand. "And you should

prepare yourself to be surprised, Ms. Brittney. Like the spaniel."

His tone conveyed gentle teasing as well as a subtle warning. The part of her that clung desperately to her good-girl core screamed out a warning to flee through the nightclub door. But the tiny sliver of her that yearned to be less like the spaniel urged her to shake his hand.

The tiny sliver won out. After all, it had good manners on its side.

She slid her hand into his, ready to give it a brief shake. But his palm was warm, his touch strong yet gentle. Once again she met his gaze and had the curious sensation of pitching forward. As if she were falling into the vast rift between the two parts of her personality.

In that instant, she knew that Connor Stone, despite his charming veneer, was a very dangerous man.

She should have run when she still had the chance.

Holding Brittney's hand, Connor felt the full force of her allure like a punch to the solar plexus. Damn. She was not just beautiful. She was knock-him-over, sexy-as-hell beautiful.

And for an instant, he wondered if she even knew it.

That look of hers was half come-hither, half pure innocence. It stirred images of tousled sheets and lazy afternoons in bed. He knew in that instant that he didn't just want to sleep with her, he wanted to pursue her. To lavish her body with sensual pleasure. To seduce her very spirit. There was something magical about her. She was the kind of woman men went to war for and wrote sonnets about.

Then he blinked and forced the moment to pass. She was just a woman. More beautiful than most, even in a city like New York, which had more than its fair share of beautiful women. But there was nothing magical, nothing sonnet-worthy. Where had *that* come from?

Feeling slightly off-kilter, he released her hand. He glanced at the dance floor, wanting to ask her to dance, but when he looked back, she was gone, retreating through the door. She'd ditched him. She'd warned him, of course, but still, it was something that rarely happened to him.

This was not how he'd imagine tonight's seduction going.

He wasn't a long-term relationship kind of guy. He drifted in and out of affairs, all with women whose expectations were as low as his. He liked an eager bedmate as much as the next guy, but work was what was important to him. Which meant he should probably be glad that Brittney Hannon had disappeared from his life as quickly as she'd appeared in it. He had neither the time nor energy for sex with a complicated woman.

Walking away now without giving her a second thought was definitely the smart move.

"Told you she'd shoot you down."

"Don't worry," he surprised himself by saying. "I'll find her again."

"Boy, you're not giving up, are you?"

"She's the daughter of a senator," Connor mused aloud. "And you said something about her going to the Hamptons for polo. How hard can she be to track down?"

"Dude, this isn't going to end with a restraining order and me being interviewed by Nancy Grace, is it?" Tim raised his hands in a gesture of innocence as Connor glared at him. "Just checking. If you're going to stalk her, I want to know in advance."

"I've never had to stalk a woman in my life." He'd meant it as a joke, but the determination in his voice surprised him.

Tim gave him an odd look. "I've never seen you like this before."

And that was precisely the problem. If he never slept with

her, Brittney would slowly become more than just a woman he'd met in a bar one night. She'd attain mythical status in his life. The woman who got away. The woman he might have written sonnets for, if he'd had the chance.

And damn it, he was not a sonnet-writing kind of guy.

No, the only solution was to find her, arrange to run into her and seduce her. Once he slept with her, he'd lose interest.

The last good girl in America was going down.

Two

What is he doing here?

Brittney could only see his profile, but she recognized Connor instantly. The VIP tent at the Clearwater Media Cup tournament was absolutely the last place she'd expected to see him. Not that she'd actually expected to see him again. Yes, two nights ago, he'd tried to pick her up in a bar. He'd even hinted that he'd surprise her with his tenacity. But surely this was just some weird fluke.

Still, it was him. That slash of ragged bangs hanging almost in his eyes was unmistakable, as were his height and commanding presence. And if he turned just ninety degrees, they'd be staring right at each other.

Coming face-to-face with Connor Stone was the last thing she wanted right now, when she was struggling to make small talk with Cynthia Rotham, one of her father's most severe critics. Pretending to fuss with her hair, Brittney shifted so her back was to him.

"Who is it?" Cynthia asked bluntly.

"What?" Brittney asked stupidly. When all else failed, feign ignorance. Not that she really believed the tactic would work. Congresswoman Rotham had made a career of feeding off of others' mistakes. The woman's vulture-like skills of observation made Brittney nervous. Brittney just knew the older woman was waiting for her to inadvertently say something stupid or offensive. Of course, the only thing worse than putting her foot in her mouth would be to say something personal that Rotham could one day use against her.

Cynthia leveled a steely gaze at her. "You spotted someone from across the tent and went white as a ghost. And now you're trying to avoid looking at him." Cynthia peered beyond Brittney's shoulder as if trying to get Connor in her sights.

"It's no one. Just someone I ran into the other night."

"Point him out. Maybe I know him."

Ha! Like she'd point Connor out to Cynthia, world-class gossip and judgmental old biddy. "I doubt that."

Brittney didn't mean to look. Really, she didn't. But just then, he laughed that throaty laugh of his. The sound of it drifted over the chatter of the crowd as if meant just for her ears. Her gaze sought him just as he raised his hand to rake his bangs off his forehead.

Beside her, Cynthia gave a sound of barely repressed glee. "Oh, my."

Brittney feigned nonchalance. "What?"

"The man who has you so disconcerted is Connor Stone. He's a hedge-fund manager." She paused, then added, grudgingly, "One of the good ones. Very reputable. Very wealthy. But I'm afraid, my dear—" Cynthia put a hand on Brittney's arm "—that he has a terrible reputation as a ladies' man."

Brittney found herself gritting her teeth so firmly she had to pry her jaws apart to speak. Returning Cynthia's false smile, she said, "You don't need to worry about me. I barely know him."

Cynthia arched a disdainful brow. "Is that so? Because I've never seen him here before. You don't suppose you made enough of an impression that he followed you here, do you?"

Yes, she wanted to say, *the other night he flirted with me so outrageously, I wanted to rip my clothes off right there in the bar.*

That would shut Rotham up. For a full ten seconds, maybe.

"Absolutely not," Brittney assured Cynthia.

"Good. Because he has a reputation for not giving up until he gets what he wants. You better hope he doesn't want you."

Cynthia looked ready to salivate at the prospect. Vulture that she was, she'd no doubt love to see Brittney's heart devoured by a world-class playboy.

Brittney wanted to tell Rotham to mind her own damn business, but that was not the way for Brittney to keep her nose clean this summer.

So instead, Brittney pretended to be thankful for the advice. "I'm sure he hasn't given me a second thought," she said with what she hoped sounded like blithe confidence.

"You'd better hope so, because he's a bit out of your league."

Brittney ignored the insult. "Now if you'll excuse me, I'm going to find a seat and watch the match. After all, though most people come here to socialize, I actually enjoy the sport."

Cynthia eyed her with anticipation. "Just be sure that's all you're enjoying."

Connor spotted Brittney just as she was leaving the VIP tent for the bleachers. The sight of her straight blond hair sent a shot of adrenaline directly to his blood. Only a few days had passed since they'd met, but he'd already spent a significant amount of time and energy researching her.

Logically he couldn't possibly expect to get as much out of the relationship as he was putting into it. In simple terms, there would not be a solid return on his investment. But it wasn't about that.

It wasn't even about the stupid bet. Though he'd used that excuse with Tim, who'd gotten him the exclusive invitation to the VIP tent. Tim was so damn convinced Connor was going to strike out that he'd actually offered to help Connor run into her again. Thanks to Tim's persistence, Connor couldn't back off even if he wanted to.

Sometimes it wasn't about the catch, it was about the chase, as his grandfather used say that. His grandfather had been a recreational fisherman—up at dawn, he'd spend hours at the lake. It was a sport Connor had never understood. All that time and energy wasted on a fish you didn't even eat. But then Connor realized his grandfather never talked about the fish he caught. But he told countless stories about the ones that got away.

If Connor let Brittney go now, he'd be admitting failure to Tim. But he'd also always wonder if he'd backed off because he thought she wasn't worth the effort—or because he was afraid she was.

He excused himself from a conversation he was having with a client. The man, the heir to a chain of drugstores, looked surprised.

"Where are you going?"

"Isn't the match about to start?" Connor asked evasively.

The client chuckled as he jostled the ice in his bourbon. "Don't tell me you actually came here to watch the matches."

Connor just smiled. "Actually, I came here to do a little fishing."

He didn't stay to see it, but he could picture the man's expression. He left the bustle of the tent and searched the crowd outside for the sight of her already-familiar blond hair. He found her immediately, even though she'd donned a wide-brimmed straw hat draped with a pale green scarf. Amid the bright and often gaudy fashion of the flashier dressers, Brittney looked elegant and delicate.

She'd jockeyed for a seat high in the bleachers and had her binoculars already out even though the ponies hadn't yet taken the field. There were several seats open around her, since most people were still in the tents.

"Mind if I sit here?" He didn't wait for a reply before taking the seat.

Her gaze jerked away from the field, her expression registering surprise as she whipped off her sunglasses to stare up at him. She opened her mouth to speak, but then snapped it shut and shoved her glasses back on.

"Not at all." She returned her attention to the field, even though the match hadn't started yet. "It's open seating. You can sit where you want."

Her tone was as cool as if she were talking to a total stranger. Which, of course, she was. The sexual tension between them was off the charts, but they still didn't know each other.

He shifted on the hard bench. Despite the fact that some of the wealthiest people in the country attended these events, the facilities were an odd mix of extravagant elegance and rugged utilitarianism. A reminder that the season was supposed to be about the sport, not just the drinks and the fashion.

"You dashed out of the tent before I had a chance to say hello."

"I like to get a good seat," she said without turning her

attention from the field where the grooms were warming up the ponies for the first chukker.

"You left quickly the other night, too. You're good at making quick exits."

Finally she looked at him. "If you're implying I'm afraid of you, you'd be wrong."

"That's good. I certainly don't want to engender fear. If you were afraid of me, I'd feel obliged to leave you alone."

She pressed her lips together in a frown, as if wishing she could back out of the conversation. He wondered if she would fake nonchalance. Finally, she seemed to decide honesty was the best policy. "I have been warned about you, you know."

"So, you were curious enough to find out who I was."

For a long moment she sat there saying nothing, the pink creeping into her cheeks the only indication she'd even heard him. "Not at all. An acquaintance pointed you out just a few minutes ago. She said you were a notorious playboy. It's not like I was asking about you."

"You're lying."

She looked at him now. Through the darkened lenses of her sunglasses, he could almost see her eyes. But not well enough to judge if she were telling the truth—or merely wished she were. "Her opinions of you were unsolicited."

He smiled. "There's no shame in doing your research. I looked you up."

"How did you know—"

"Who you were? Turns out you're fairly recognizable. Brittney Hannon, Last Good Girl in America."

Her mouth snapped shut. He could nearly hear her teeth grinding down.

"I take it you didn't like that profile."

"If we had a week, I couldn't tell you all the things wrong with that glib assessment of my personality. How would you like to be summed up in a single catchy phrase for all of America?"

"A single phrase like 'notorious playboy'? At least they gave you six words. You only gave me two."

"Those were her words, not mine," she protested.

Still, he got the reaction he was hoping for: a wry smile and a voice filled with chagrin. "I'm sure you're more than just a workaholic playboy."

"I got workaholic, too?"

"It doesn't change anything." There was a glimmer of what might have been regret in her gaze. "You and I, we don't match."

He nearly chuckled at her straightforward honesty. It was hard not to admire that. "I think we'd match quite nicely."

He drew out the words, giving her imagination time to kick in—just as his had. She'd crossed her legs away from him when he'd first sat down, which had made her dress inch up, revealing a tempting stretch of thigh. Now, she shifted in her seat, obviously aware he was looking at her. The lovely pink of her cheeks deepened. "That's not what I meant."

"Of course."

"But it proves my point perfectly. You're all sexual innuendo and I'm...not. With me, what you see is what you get."

"That doesn't mean we can't be together."

"You're right. That doesn't. But there are plenty of other things that do. If you'd really done your research, you'd know that."

"Oh, I did my research."

"Did you actually read the profile?"

"That's where I started."

She uncrossed her legs, shifting toward him in her seat. "Then you know—"

"No one's that good. Besides, I was there the other night." That tempting stretch of thigh was even closer. He leaned forward, bracing his forearms on his knees, bringing his hands mere inches from her skin. No one observing them would notice—they'd just look like two people having an intense conversation. "You can't deny you're attracted to me."

"I'm not trying to," she said.

Her gaze was as direct as her words. With her, there were no attempts at deception.

He brushed his knuckle across the skin of her outer leg, just above her knee. A tiny, subtle gesture. He expected her to move away from his touch. When she didn't, a jolt of pleasure coursed through him. She hadn't taken the bait, but she wasn't swimming in the other direction either.

"I tempt you." He let his knuckle circle over her skin in a slow, lazy motion. "For all your talk about abstinence, you nearly let a stranger pick you up in a bar the other night."

He was surprised that she met his gaze head on. Her eyes were wide, her pupils dilated. Her breath was coming in slow draws that were too even to be anything other than forced. He was getting to her. But she wasn't letting herself be intimidated by his overt pursuit. Damn, but he liked her.

After a moment, her gaze hardened. "You really want to debate abstinence with the last good girl in America?"

He nearly chuckled. "I can think of things I'd rather do with you. But I'll settle for talking."

"Talking is all you're going to get."

"I'll take my chances, because whatever you claim to believe about chastity, you wish you could give in."

"But I won't. That's the point." She jolted to her feet, shoving her binoculars into her oversized bag. "Come on, then."

He stood. "Where are we going?"

"Away from here." She scanned their surroundings. "This is the opening match of the Clearwater Tournament. There are more celebrities here than on Broadway, which means it's the most photographed, talked about, gossiped about event of the season. I'm not going to sit here in plain sight of five hundred cameras and microphones and debate my morals with you."

"So we're going somewhere more private? You have a hell of a way of turning a man down."

Brittney led Connor down the bleacher steps, through the throng of people to the very edge of the field, where the crowd tapered off to a mere trickle. Gradually, the rows and rows of horse trailers gave way to open pasture divided by split-rail fences. Nestled against the tree line sat the massive barn dating back to Seven Oaks's midcentury days as a dairy farm. The odd groom wandered past, but they were far enough from the crowds that they were essentially alone.

They walked toward the old dairy barn, with its gambrel roof and icon silo towering behind it. Whenever they were within earshot of others, she narrated their progress with the history of Seven Oaks Farms and of the Clearwater Media Tournament. On the few occasions when someone stopped to greet her, she made a point of introducing Connor and explaining his recent interest in the sport. Anyone who overheard their conversation would probably pity Connor. But he showed no signs of boredom.

Her heart pounded in her chest, issuing a frantic warning: *Turn back now! This is a mistake!*

Nevertheless, she kept her hands firmly clasped in front of her, speaking partly to calm her fears and partly to dissuade him. "The thing about you, Connor, is you think you're going to get my attention by being shocking, but the truth is I've met men like you before."

"I doubt that."

"I know your type," she told him as they walked. "You've decided I'm a challenge. A prize to be won. You probably have some fishing or hunting metaphor you're using." She slanted a look at him from under her lashes, trying to gauge how close she was to hitting the mark, but he kept his expression carefully blank. A sure sign she was right. Dang it.

She didn't *want* to be right about this. Some tiny—stupid—part of her wanted him to deny it. When he didn't, she continued. "But I'm not worried. You'll lose interest as soon as you realize I'm not going to be easy to bag. Or whatever metaphor is suitable."

He stopped walking, forcing her to stop as well. She turned back to face him, only to find him studying her with that disconcerting intensity. His gaze felt heavy with appreciation. But unlike most men who gave her body heated glances, he was looking into her eyes. As if it were her thoughts that interested him, not her curves.

"I think," he stated baldly, "that you underestimate my endurance and my creativity."

And there it was again. That innuendo that sent tendrils of heat pulsing through her body. The man was too tempting by a mile. She could only pray that she *wasn't* underestimating him. If he was half as creative as he claimed, she was in serious trouble. Who was she kidding? She'd *been* in serious trouble from the moment they'd met.

Which was why she had to nip this in the bud. He made her want to give in to temptation. And that simply wasn't something she could afford to do. If her assessment of his motives was dead on—and she'd bet it was—then she was nothing more than a challenge to him. Something to accomplish. She wasn't willing to bargain away her morals for that, no matter how pleasurable the experience might be.

Intellectually, she knew that. It was her body she was having trouble convincing.

Which was why she couldn't risk having him pursue her for very long. What if her hormones overran her otherwise very logical mind? This had to stop. Unfortunately, the only way she could think of to deter him was with brutal honesty.

"Maybe I have underestimated you," she began, "but you have definitely underestimated me. My ideas about abstinence aren't something I came up with on a whim. I'm not a virginal teenage girl who's made a well-meaning but misguided pledge. I'm an adult woman. I know what I'm talking about."

His hands were tucked in his pockets. The heated look he gave her seemed to see into her very soul. In that instant, she could have sworn he could read her mind.

"And what exactly are your views about sex?"

She narrowed her gaze at him. "You said you read the article."

"Maybe I want to hear them straight from you."

"Or maybe you just want to hear me talk about sex."

His lips twitched. "Can you blame me?"

She sighed, trying not to let her exasperation get the better of her. Unless she got this out on the table, he'd never believe she really meant it. Maybe she'd even forget that she really meant it.

They'd wandered far enough from the field that they were truly alone. She had orchestrated this very situation, getting him alone so that she could be blunt without being overheard.

Plus, she figured there was a good chance her honesty would be a turnoff for him. That was certainly the case with the last man she'd dated seriously. Phillip Gould, a young congressman from Virginia—who'd been her father's protégé, in addition to being her boyfriend. Their relationship had ended badly. She wouldn't tolerate his cheating and—it turned out—he couldn't tolerate hardly anything about her. It seemed their mutual desire to impress her father had been all that they had in common.

During their last big fight, Philip had called her tedious

and a bore. Dull. Of course those men she'd dated since that blasted profile had found her opinions equally tedious. Maybe Connor would agree. Which would be a good thing. Right?

Yet now that it came down to it, she found herself reluctant to speak her views aloud. Which was odd because she'd never felt that way in the past. Or maybe she'd simply never before been in the position of talking about sex with someone to whom she was attracted.

"It's simple." Her words came in fits and starts. "I think women today sell themselves short. Real relationships take work, and a commitment from both the man and the woman. One-night stands are easy. But they're less enjoyable."

"I think that depends on who you have the one-night stand with."

"Well, sure, if you're a man," she countered. "A man can enjoy sex with anyone. It's more complicated for a woman."

"That's an oversimplification."

She shook her head. "I don't think so." Her words came more quickly as she warmed to her subject. "For a man, pleasure is straightforward. Orgasms are easy. It's not like that for a woman. Unless you're both emotionally involved, it's too easy for a man to take his pleasure and ignore a woman's needs. One-night stands aren't fulfilling, emotionally or physically."

"And you're speaking from experience?"

"I'm right," she said finally. "I know I'm right."

"How could you possibly know you're right when your theories have never been tested?"

"I'm not a complete innocent. I do have experience with men."

"So I suppose there are legions of men who weren't able to satisfy you."

She tried to glare at him despite her amusement. "You make me sound like a tramp on a warpath to punish men because they couldn't make me climax. Sex is more complicated than that."

"Was it legions or wasn't it?" he prodded, his tone gently teasing. "You can't be experienced and innocent. You can't have it both ways."

In that moment, under the heat of his steady gaze, she remembered a crucial detail. This wasn't a philosophical discussion. It wasn't a discussion at all. It was a seduction. And she was no longer holding her own against him.

"I have experience," she insisted. "Enough to know that I'm right."

"Okay, then," he agreed way too easily. "I'm sure you're right." Connor paused strategically, slanting her a look. "Just out of curiosity, who were these men?"

She scoffed, but trepidation was creeping behind her bravado. "You know I'm not going to answer that."

"Why not? It's only fair. You're shooting me down without giving me a chance because of some mysterious men in your past whom you found disappointing. If I'm going to be judged based on their bad performances, I should at least know who they are."

"Don't be ridiculous." She had such trouble reading him: was he just an arrogant jerk trying to get into her pants or was he just teasing her? She couldn't tell.

They'd reached the line of trees that ran along the edge of the property from the dairy barn to the main house. The soft whispering of the breeze through the willows and oaks almost drowned out the faint murmur of the crowd in the distance. A few more steps and the barn would block their view of the polo field.

Her heart rate picked up, and she wasn't sure if it was from the urge to run or the desire twirling through her belly.

She was about to flee toward the field when he snagged her hand and pulled her to a stop.

"Come on, I should know their names, these guys who are so bad in bed they've ruined you for other men."

"I never said—"

"What if one of them is dating my sister?"

She gave her hand a light tug, but he didn't release it. His palm felt warm against hers, and she didn't have the heart to wrest it from his. She smiled, bemused by her own reaction and by him. "Do you even have a sister?"

"Not the point." As he spoke, he started walking toward the barn, her hand neatly tucked in his. "It could be someone I know. Unless you give me some names, I won't know whom to trust. What if it's my best friend?"

This time she laughed out loud. "I seriously doubt that you're best friends with my prom date."

He stopped in his tracks. "Your prom date?" His face registered exaggerated surprise. "We're talking about your prom date here? We've gone from legions of men who've disappointed you in bed to a single, overeager teenage boy?"

From another man, the teasing might have offended her, but he did it in such a gentle way, she found herself laughing at her own foibles. "I never said legions. That was your word."

"But he was a teenager. You're assuming you know how I'm going to be in bed based on the experience of one boy?"

"It wasn't just *one* boy."

"I can't help but notice you emphasized 'one' in that sentence, not 'boy.' Which means we're still talking about boys here."

She felt the trap he'd been setting begin to close around her, finally giving her the strength to tug her hand free and walk away from him. "So?" she asked.

"Back when you were a kid, you had a couple of tumbles with teenagers and they couldn't satisfy you. So you developed this harebrained theory of yours."

"It's not a harebrained theory." *Is it?*

"It's not a statistically valid one."

She turned to face him. She didn't want to mention Phillip, who had not been a teenage boy at all but a full-grown man. In that case, she hadn't been the only one dissatisfied, so it hardly seemed part of the argument.

"What's your point?"

"My point is, you're not being fair." Before she could protest, he continued. "You're not being logical either. You've based all your assumptions about one-night stands on your experience with teenage boys."

"So?" she prodded again.

He chuckled gently. With two quick steps he had her backed up against the wall of the barn. He braced a hand by her shoulder and leaned toward her. In the dappled light streaming down through the trees, his expression was hungry. Predatory, but not cruel.

"Teenage boys," he said, "have no self-control and very little experience. Which means they don't know what they're doing."

His words left no doubt. He would know what he was doing. With Connor, there would be no awkward fumbling. No mumbled apologies. There would be only pleasure. Her whole body shuddered, and she had to bite down on her lip to hide it.

"If you really want to be fair, you have to test your theories. Not with a boy. With a man."

Her gaze met his. She knew what was going through his mind as clearly as if his imagination was projecting onto a movie screen behind him. He was picturing them in bed together. His body moving over hers. Into hers.

She sucked in a deep breath. "So what do you suggest? That I sleep with you, just so you can prove your point?" She tried to scoff, but her words came out too high-pitched.

He studied her face carefully. She had the impression he was trying to decide if she was the kind of woman who would back down from a challenge. "You can walk away from me right now. Maybe I'll even just let you go. Or maybe you're right and I'll get bored and stop pursuing you eventually. But the truth is, if that does happen, then all you'll have gained is the knowledge that you were more stubborn. Not that you were right."

"You're still suggesting I sleep with you just so you can prove your point."

He ran his hand up her arm. "No, I'm suggesting you just give me a chance. A single kiss. That's all I'm asking." He moved his thumb from the top of her arm to the underside, tracing a circle along the tender skin there. "You stop me whenever you want. If I'm wrong, you'll be completely unaffected by our kiss."

Her gaze skittered back to his. Her chest was rising and falling in short staccato bursts. Had he noticed? Did he know how aroused she was when he'd barely even touched her? "And if you're right?"

"All I'm asking is that you give me a try. One kiss. What harm can I do with just one kiss?"

She tilted her head to the side, considering her options. "Why is one kiss so important to you?"

"Why are you working so hard to avoid giving me one? What are you afraid will happen if you give in?"

She couldn't afford to be honest with him. *I'm afraid I'll lose control completely. I'm afraid I'll have no restraint.*

"Just one kiss?" she asked.

"I'll stop the moment you ask me to," he said evasively.

"Do you promise?"

"Absolutely."

Three

Connor knew he could afford to promise, because he knew she wouldn't ask him to stop.

He considered her for a moment. Between her wide-brimmed hat and oversized sunglasses, she had more body armor than a warrior about to go into battle. Without even touching her skin, he gave the end of her scarf a long, slow tug. When the knot released, he gently removed her hat. Of course, then he was stuck holding the ridiculous thing. Luckily, a tree branch hung nearby and he dangled it from the end. As for her glasses, he raised them to the top of her head.

When he looked at her again, he smiled. Her cheeks were flushed, her chest rising and failing rapidly. She was in expert hands now and she knew it.

He stood perfectly still, one hand on her arm, the other on the wall beside her, waiting for her to give the go-ahead before pulling her into his arms. She moved before he had a chance to, rising on her toes and pressing her chest against his. He barely noticed her bag dropping to the ground. Her hands burrowed into his hair, angling his head to meet her lips.

Everything about the kiss surprised him, from the way she took full command to the scorching heat of her mouth.

After all her talk of propriety and abstinence, he expected timidity. He thought that he'd have to be the aggressor, that he'd have to gently tease a response out of her. Instead, it was the opposite. Her kiss was bold, if a bit clumsy. Completely enchanting.

Her hands clung to him as her tongue traced the crease of his lips. She didn't have to ask twice. He opened his mouth to her, nearly shuddering with desire when her tongue darted into his mouth, eager and fast, like a ravenous hummingbird. He realized then how quickly this could get out of hand. She had it in her to dominate her lover completely. An inexperienced man might mistake her natural enthusiasm for arousal. Or worse, be so turned on that he couldn't wait for her. If she'd been like this at eighteen, no wonder the poor guys hadn't lasted.

He moved his own hands to the sides of her face and pulled his mouth from hers. She tried to follow him, rising higher onto her to toes. He nudged her down with his hands on her shoulders, pressing his forehead to hers.

"Slow down. It's not a race."

She pulled back, blinking as if dazed. He knew how she felt.

"Give me a second and then let's try this again." He sucked in a deep breath. The smell of her flooded his senses, sweet and somehow homey, with just a hint of citrus. Like lemon cookies. His favorite.

When he heard her breath slow down, he lowered his mouth back to hers, taking control, coaxing her mouth open, moving his tongue against hers in slow, sensuous strokes. Her body relaxed against his and he set about seducing her with his kiss. He'd promised her he'd stop the minute she asked, and he would. He just had to make sure she didn't ask. He wouldn't push her for more than she was willing to give. No, if there was going beyond a single kiss, she'd have to take it there.

And she did. Sooner than he thought, her hands were moving down his chest, tugging the hem of his shirt free from his pants. He sucked in a breath as her palm reached the bare skin of his abdomen. Her fingers were cool, her touch light and fluttering.

He might not have intended to push her, but turnabout was fair play. She was dressed in a simple wraparound dress, which made it all too easy to slip his hand into her bodice. All he wanted was to touch her bare skin, but she misinterpreted his actions and moved his hand to the tie at her waist. With a single tug of her fingers, her dress fell open. His surprise nearly knocked him off his feet. They were alone, but they were still outside.

He glanced down. The sight of her sent desire rocketing through him. The way the fabric of her dress fell across the sides of her body, the way her hot-pink bra encased the pale, creamy skin of her breasts. And, my God, that bra.

Because she dressed so conservatively, he'd thought he might have to brave a fortress of starchy white nylon to reach her skin. Instead, she'd shocked him with scanty silk and lace. It was a fantasy come to life. A miracle of engineering in fuchsia. He really could write a sonnet about the things that bra did.

What the hell was the Last Good Girl in America doing wearing a bra and panties like that?

Somehow the combination of hot-pink silk and her naked flesh in the dappled light was almost too much. She was too perfect, with the bright afternoon sun filtering down through the leaves of the tree, making her bare skin glimmer. He wanted to drop to his knees and worship her.

This was not how it was supposed to happen. He'd planned on seducing her. Pushing her to her limits. Not the other way around. That's when it hit him. He was in serious trouble. And he didn't even give a damn.

Watching the desire flicker across Connor's face, a surge of pure feminine power shot through Brittney.

She'd always known men found her attractive. A body like hers was designed to bring men to their knees. She knew that in the same way she understood foreign trade agreements—dispassionately. As if it were unrelated to her personally. It was like owning a chain saw but never choosing to use it. Why would she? She didn't need to chop down any trees.

But watching Connor's reaction to her body, for the first time, she felt the power of it. This man, this notorious playboy, whose affairs were so legendary people had warned her about him…he wanted her.

She saw it in his face more clearly than he could have told her with a thousand seductive murmurings. His reaction to her filled her with power. And his desire surprised him, too. She also read that in his expression. He was shaken by how much he wanted her. And she'd never seen anything more erotic in her life than that mixture of shock and raw lust.

Need shot through her, zinging every nerve in her body with energy. Her fingers trembled with eagerness as she shimmied out of her dress. A breeze drifted from under the tree, tantalizing her skin as her dress fluttered to the ground, leaving her clad only in her bra and panties.

For a moment, Connor merely stood there, his gaze raking over her exposed body. Then he smiled, looking like a kid on Christmas morning, set loose in FAO Schwartz. Brittney was damn glad that the lingerie she'd always considered her private indulgence was not so private now.

He closed the distance between them, pressing his body to hers, and thoughts of everyone and everything else vanished. Her skin felt overly sensitized, every nerve ending aware of the brush of his hands and the grazing of his clothes. He was still fully dressed and her hands tugged at buttons and fabric, desperate to level the playing field, to expose the smooth expanse of his skin to her touch.

His hands were hot and needy, one cupping her breast, the other her backside. He hitched her up, wedging a leg between hers. The pressure at the juncture of her thighs was an exquisite torture. She rocked her hips forward and back, shuddering with pleasure. His mouth nipped at her neck while he thumbed her nipple through her bra, matching the rhythm of her movements.

She felt her nerves tightening, an orgasm just out of her reach. Sucking in deep breaths, she tried to stay in front of it. "Please, Connor," she gasped, "tell me you have a condom."

"I do."

She was only vaguely aware of him fumbling for it. A moment later, he was thumbing aside the fabric of her thong and thrusting into her. He kept his fingers right at her juncture, rubbing the apex of her desire, pushing her over the edge as he reached his own climax, buried deep inside of her.

It wasn't supposed to be like this.

Connor'd had it all planned out. He'd sleep with her. Get her out of his system. Move on.

He wasn't supposed to lose control. *She* was.

Knowing that they'd both lost control was little consolation.

Her body was still trembling as he pulled away from her. Heart pounding, he straightened his clothes. And then picked up her dress. He scrubbed a hand through his hair and down his face. Picking her dress up off the ground was almost as disconcerting as taking it off had been. Nothing about Brittney was what he expected.

She blinked lazily, her expression dazed, her cheeks flushed, her lips swollen and red. Anyone who so much as glanced at her would know she'd just been taken up against a wall. Everything about her was erotic and tempting.

So much so that the sight of her might have turned him on all over again. If he hadn't just had the most fantastic orgasm of his life. And if he weren't fighting back panic. He got her back into her dress as quickly as he could.

She smiled up at him with dazzling trust. "That was amazing." Her hands fluttered to her hair and then to her chest, like she was trying to keep her heart from pounding out of it. "Is it always like that?" Then she laughed as she knotted the ties on her dress. "I mean, I know it's supposed to be good. But I had no idea…"

The tie of her dress was still askance. He reached to straighten it, but the small effort did little to help. "We've got to get you out of here. What's the fastest way back to the parking lot, where we won't see anyone?"

"Back behind the barn, I think." She looked confused. "Should we leave?"

"Definitely." He gripped her elbow and steered her in the opposite direction of the field.

"Can we do it again?" Her breath seemed to catch with excitement. She laughed again, that low, sexy rumble that stirred parts of him that had no business stirring. "Gosh, I sound so naive, don't I? I just—"

He cut her off, muttering a curse under his breath. "Let's just get out of here."

For several steps, she walked along beside him. Then she stumbled, and he could almost feel her tension building.

Suddenly she dug in her heels and stopped. "You're ditching me already, aren't you."

"I'm not ditching you," he countered quickly. Never mind that logic dictated honesty would be the best approach here. She looked too hurt for him to go with honesty. So he hedged. "I'm going to take you home. You said yourself you didn't want any gossip. If anyone saw you looking like this, there'd be talk."

She held up her palms as if warding off an attack. "Hey, it's okay. I get it." Her gaze traveled the length of his body, and he had the uneasy sensation she'd summed up the breadth of his soul, as well. "This is the kind of guy you are." Her lips curved in a wry, self-deprecating smile. "I knew it going in. I was warned. I saw it coming from a mile away. And I still fell for it. My mistake."

Her arms wrapped around her waist and she brushed past, heading for her car without looking back.

Let her go, his logical mind demanded. *Just let her walk away. That'll be easiest on everyone.*

And, damn it, that's what he would have done. If she hadn't paused and turned back to deliver one last barb.

"And for those in the audience keeping score, I won this point. Even when the sex is good, it's still not worth it."

With that she turned and walked away.

He wanted to let her go, wanted to pretend that he hadn't hurt her, that he wasn't acting like a complete ass.

But he knew he was.

"Wait a second," he called out, speeding up to catch her. "You're not even giving me a chance."

She eyed him shrewdly. "A chance to what? Dump me in a more humiliating manner?"

There was such vulnerability in her gaze, along with a liberal dash of sass. Before logic had a chance to beat him over the head again, he turned her to face him and cupped her face in his hand. "Look, I have a client I have to see tonight." The lie slipped out cleanly. "But I'll see you tomorrow."

Her gaze was suspicious. "You don't really want to see me. You're just feeling guilty."

"I do," he argued. "Promise me you'll meet me somewhere."

Now he was begging her to meet him? How the hell had *that* happened?

She bit down on her lower lip as she considered her options.

"Let me take you to dinner," he offered.

Finally she shook her head, pulling away from him. "No. Tomorrow night is the Harbor Lights Gala for the local schools. I was on the planning committee for years. If I miss the event, people will notice."

"I'll meet you there."

Her expression was blank, but he could tell she was struggling to keep it that way. He walked her the rest of the way to her car, wishing he had a better handle on her emotions. Or, for that matter, on his own.

She swung the door open but paused before climbing in. When she spoke, her tone was even, all traces of suspicion gone. "Look, it's fine. I knew exactly what I was getting into. You didn't mislead me."

There it was again. That blunt honesty. Her gaze met his, her blue eyes almost painfully clear of accusation.

"Brit..." he began, but he didn't know how to finish the sentence. She so clearly saw through all his crap. And she was giving him a chance to walk away. Guilt-free.

Before he had a chance to stop himself, he brushed a hand up her arm to her shoulder. He pulled her to him, intending to simply hug her. But at the last second, her face turned up to his and he found himself unable to resist the lure of that tempting mouth. His lips found hers, coaxing them open with the gentlest of touches.

All those things he couldn't say, all those emotions he couldn't even name, he poured them into the kiss. The regret, the apology, even the fear. The sheer awe he felt at her stunning mix of innocence, honesty and sensuality.

She leaned into him and kissed him with knee-weakening passion. He felt the tendrils of her desire taking root deep within him as she arched her body against his, sliding a leg up along the outside of his thigh. It took every ounce of his self-control to break the kiss.

By the time he lifted his mouth, he could see he'd kissed away the last of her suspicion. As she climbed into her car and drove away, Connor was mentally kicking himself. He'd made things worse, not better.

Brittney should send him running for the hills. Yet he'd just promised to see her again. Begged for it, actually. What was it about this woman that turned him into a total idiot?

Four

Once, as a teenager, in a brief burst of curiosity about the mother who had left her, Brittney had spent hours at the local library reading interviews with Kandy Hannon. Most were from the time immediately after her scandalous affair and marriage to Brittney's father, the then-freshman senator. In those articles, her words were carefully guarded and most likely well rehearsed. But in the few interviews she'd done after leaving her husband and abandoning her three-year-old daughter, Kandy Hannon spoke freely.

To the teenage Brittney, the most memorable quote was, "Why on earth would I be ashamed of having sex? It's great exercise and makes my skin glow. Why not enjoy it as often as I can?"

For a brief time, Brittney flirted with adopting that philosophy for herself. She hadn't enjoyed it. At all. Since then, she'd eschewed her mother's ideas about sex in favor of her own, very conservative views.

One afternoon with Connor had changed all that. Despite her doubts about his intentions, she woke up the next morning with a feeling of smug contentment. She felt more in control of her sexuality than ever before. It almost didn't matter if he showed up at the gala. Her body hummed, her mind buzzed and her skin glowed. For the first time in her life, she felt like she really was the daughter of Kandy Hannon.

And it was all thanks to Connor and the miraculous things he'd done to her body.

He might not show up to the gala this evening, and if he didn't, she'd survive. One more life lesson learned.

But if he did show up, what then? Yesterday, she'd been unable to tell if he was motivated by guilt or if he genuinely wanted to see her again. She'd have to play it by ear.

That should be no problem. After all, she'd lived her entire life in the limelight of her father's political career, playing things by ear. If she could figure out how to get through dinner with the president and first lady at age twelve, she could darn well run into Connor at a gala. She'd made it through that crucial dinner, despite the nausea clutching her stomach, by taking tiny bites and smiling a lot. She'd do the same tonight.

Funny how much of her life she spent thinking about a woman she hadn't even seen since she was three. After abandoning her husband and daughter, Kandy had spent a few years stirring up trouble and living recklessly. She'd died in a skiing accident when Brittney was ten.

Though Brittney barely remembered her, Kandy had left an indelible mark on her life. They looked so much alike, Brittney felt as though everything her mother had done was a reflection on her. Between dodging her mother's past and trying not to impinge on her father's future, sometimes Brittney felt as though she barely had a life of her own. Until yesterday, in Connor's presence, when she'd forgotten both.

She spent an unproductive day trying not to think about Connor. By late afternoon, when it was time for her to dress for the gala, she was tired of contemplating her future. She was ready to simply be done with the evening.

She was prepared to face whatever met her. Except for what was actually there.

Connor stayed in his room at the B&B where he was staying for most of the day, catching up on world news and his backlog of e-mail on his laptop. He'd even downloaded an action flick and watched that. Anything to keep his mind off Brittney. He also did the unthinkable and kept his phone off. When he finally turned it on, he saw he'd received no fewer than seven phone calls from Tim.

As much as he wanted to avoid talking to anyone, he figured he had no choice but to return the call.

"Connor," Tim said as soon as he picked up, "did I underestimate you."

"What are you talking about?"

"When you said you'd get her into bed within the week, I thought you were full of it. Man, was I wrong. What can I say, other than I owe you a thousand bucks?"

Anxiety clutched at Connor's chest. He repeated his question slowly. "What. Are. You. Talking. About?"

"Brittney Hannon. You and her hooking up. That picture of you two on Headin-for-the-Hamptons.com was smoking hot."

Great.

Connor hung up on Tim. By the time he'd set down his iPhone, he was already loading the Web site. And there it was on the front page of the site's coverage of the polo tournament.

There were actually two pictures. The first was a grainy black-and-white photo that had to be at least thirty years old. A young Senator Hannon, dressed in a suit and looking clean-cut, with a blonde bombshell pressed against him in the risqué costume of an Atlantic City showgirl, her naked limbs entwined with his. The photo's combination of disheveled business suit and bare skin suggested an illicit embrace.

Connor had seen it before, when he'd searched Google for Brittney after meeting her. It was the photo that had nearly ruined the senator's career.

But it wasn't nearly as shocking as the photo beside it.

The second photo also portrayed a well-dressed man and a scantily clad blonde bombshell. But unlike the first photo, this one was in garish bright color. And it wasn't nearly thirty years old. It was less than twenty-four hours old.

It was a photo of Connor and Brittney, kissing outside her car in the parking lot at the match, her hair mussed, her clothing disheveled.

How the hell had they gotten that shot?

His breath came in short, ragged gusts as he fought to control his anger. His mind raced. He'd find out whoever was responsible. He'd have him fired. He'd sue him. Crush him financially. Hell, he'd kill him.

The prospect of some nameless member of the paparazzi lying trampled under the hooves of polo horses made Connor feel only marginally better. Only once his vision began to clear did he read the headline spanning the width of the two pictures.

Looks Like The Apple Doesn't Fall Far From The Tree!

He quickly scanned the article. Straight gossip would have been bad enough, but the site aimed well below the belt. It liberally referenced the interview that had run in *New York Personality*. Worse still, it implied Brittney only pretended to practice abstinence to pacify her father's constituents while actually sleeping around.

He cursed as he dug through his pocket for his car keys. It wasn't the papparazzi who deserved to die painfully. It was him.

The whispers of gossip were especially fierce when Brittney arrived at the Harbor Lights Gala on Sunday evening. She didn't pay any mind to the murmurs. Until she noticed that stares of barely veiled curiosity were pointed at her.

First it was just a glance here and there. The glare of a matronly older woman. The nervous snicker of a teenage boy who held her gaze too long. The knowing smile and faint nod of a woman who was known for her sexual escapades. But it was the lewd "Hey, baby" grin of a guy in his twenties that made the hair on the back of her neck prickle.

Suddenly nervous, she scanned the crowd, looking for a friendly face. She'd been socializing with some of these people for most of her life. But the only person who looked approachable at the moment was Vanessa Hughes. Though she and Vanessa had never been close, they'd been acquaintances for years. Vanessa shot her a look full of sympathy that made the bottom drop out of Brittney's stomach. Whatever was going on, Vanessa knew about it.

Brittney quickly crossed the lawn to Vanessa. As always, the beautiful blonde was dressed impeccably in a white sundress, her oversized sunglasses propped on her head. As if they were far closer than they actually were, Brittney gave Vanessa a quick buss on the cheek and then linked arms with her.

"Protect me from the circling vultures?" she asked under her breath.

Vanessa picked up Brittney's cue and smiled cheerfully. "Absolutely." Softly she added, "Am I wrong in thinking you don't yet know why the vultures are circling?"

Brittney's smile felt tight as she shook her head.

In a voice loud enough for passersby to hear, Vanessa said, "You've got to try these canapés." She guided Brittney to the edge of the lawn where the catering tents were set up. As they walked, Vanessa pulled her iPhone out of her enormous Jimmy Choo bag and surreptitiously pulled up a Web page. She slipped the phone into Brittney's hand as she loaded up a plate with appetizers.

Brittney recognized the Headin' for the Hamptons site. Then the world fell away as she saw the pictures. Her blood pounded through her head—all she heard was a distant roaring. She had to concentrate to read the headline. As bad as the photos were, the accompanying article was even worse.

One bad choice, one little mistake, and everything she'd ever stood for was in question. A single scandalous photo wouldn't be so bad for the average politician's daughter. But she'd always been so vocal about abstinence. Her entire adult life, she'd advocated women respecting themselves enough to eschew promiscuity and find committed, long-term relationships.

The Web site made sure to point that out. It made it sound as though she'd said those things merely to pander to her father's more conservative voters, while she was partying and sleeping around with men she barely knew.

And the horrible truth was, it was right. She had betrayed everything she believed in for a few minutes of mindless pleasure in the arms of a man she barely knew.

"I can't…" she muttered under her breath, but the sentence died in her mouth before she could finish it. Panic tightened around her throat, making speech impossible.

Beside her, Vanessa threw back her head and laughed, like she'd said something outrageously funny.

Stung, Brittney just gaped at her.

Vanessa gave Brittney's arm a gentle squeeze. "If they know it hurts you, it makes the feeding frenzy worse."

Brittney nodded in understanding. Vanessa had always had a reputation as a wild child. Just last summer, Vanessa had had a tumultuous fling with polo player Nicolas Valera. There'd been gossip aplenty about that.

Taking advice from someone who'd weathered her share of storms, Brittney gave a trembling smile. "Right. Thank you. I—"

She broke off as she glimpsed Connor watching her from across the lawn. She didn't have a chance to read his expression because suddenly Cynthia Rotham was bearing down on her.

"Well, well, well," Cynthia practically cooed with glee, "if it isn't the Last Good Girl in America."

Brittney's panic hardened into resolve. She refused to be cowed by Cynthia Rotham. "You know, I'm really starting to hate that title."

"Don't worry, darling, you've already lost it." The veil of kindness dropped from Cynthia's face as she leaned forward. "I'm surprised you had the guts to show your face today. You always struck me as such a spineless creature, not good for much but looking demure in pictures. Yet here you are. I can't decide if it's admirable or stupid."

Cynthia's arrogance was almost too much to bear.

Vanessa tried to wedge herself between Brittney and Cynthia like a human shield. "Why don't you go spew your venom on someone else?"

Cynthia glared at Vanessa. "Ah, Vanessa. Are you two friends all of a sudden? Do we have your influence to thank for Brittney's new loose morals?"

Brittney wasn't about to let Cynthia verbally knock Vanessa around. "I make my own decisions and my own mistakes. So back off."

"This was more than a mistake." She let loose a cackling laugh. "Little Miss Prim and Proper was caught with a man she barely knows. The backlash will do wonders for your father's career."

Brittney swayed. Hearing her worst fears voiced aloud made her light-headed. But before she could voice a rebuttal, she felt a hand on her elbow. She knew in an instant who it was.

Connor.

At the soothing stroke of his hand on her arm and the faint whiff of his scent—woodsy and masculine—something inside of her relaxed.

He extended a hand to Cynthia. "I don't think we've met. Brittney hasn't had time to introduce me to all of her friends yet."

Cynthia narrowed her gaze suspiciously. And didn't take his hand.

He left his hand in midair, all but forcing Cynthia to extend her own.

As he shook her hand, he added, "I'm Connor Stone. Brittney's fiancé."

Beside him, Connor felt Brittney tense. She might have been turned to stone. He could only hope her larynx was frozen as well. If he was going to throw himself under the bus to save her, he damn well didn't want her blocking his dive.

He talked fast, not giving the women a chance to speak. "Boy, we got caught, didn't we? Here we were, trying to hide our relationship just a little bit longer, and we goofed." He squeezed Brittney's shoulder. "Brit, why don't you introduce me to your friends?"

He recognized Vanessa Hughes, of course. Since she was standing shoulder to shoulder with Brittney, he assumed they were friends. The older woman, on the other hand, was clearly little more than a vulture come to feast on a scandal.

Brittney recovered first. "Connor, this is Cynthia

Rotham." Then she cleared her throat. "*Congresswoman* Rotham, that is."

Ah. That explained her obvious panic as well as the woman's rapacious expression. From what he understood, Congresswoman Rotham was one of Brittney's father's most vocal opponents.

He squeezed Brittney's shoulder while giving Cynthia his best smile. "I think people will forgive us for kissing in public, once they see how in love we are."

Cynthia scoffed. "Kissing? Is that what it was?"

Connor leveled his gaze at the older woman. "A man's still allowed to kiss his fiancée in public, isn't he?"

She ignored the quiet warning in his tone. "If you really are engaged."

Brittney opened her mouth to speak but Connor didn't give her the chance. "If it were up to me, we'd be married already."

Vanessa's lips twitched in an effort to suppress laughter.

Connor smiled broadly and said, "Now, if you'll excuse us, Brittney promised to introduce me to all the movers and shakers here."

As he took Brittney's arm and led her away, he thought he heard the congresswoman gasp at the implication that she wasn't important enough to count as one of those movers and shakers.

As soon as they were out of earshot, Brittney whispered, "Fiancé? What were you thinking, claiming to be my fiancé?"

She seemed unaware of the eyes still following them. He gave her arm a squeeze. He'd been squeezing a lot of her body parts this evening, and none of the good ones.

"Smile," he muttered under his breath. "The congresswoman isn't watching just now, but a lot of other people are."

She didn't miss a beat, quickly fixing a pleasant expression on her face. But her tone betrayed her arrogance. "What the hell are you doing?"

Man, she was good. Years of living in the public eye had apparently honed her ability to hide her true emotions.

He cut straight to the chase. "That picture was a disaster. For you, not me. I'm barely visible in the photo, and other than my elderly grandmother who will probably rip me a new one, no one cares what I do or who I sleep with."

"That's a nice image. Thanks for that."

"You, on the other hand, are easily recognizable. And correct me if I'm wrong, but isn't it an election year for your father? Which means that photo—"

"You don't have to tell me what it means," she snapped. They'd reached the edge of the lawn. In the dusk, lights strung along the tents glistened off the water, casting the harbor in a glow of warm light. She was obviously in no mood to enjoy any of it.

Keenly aware they were still the objects of curious stares, he settled his hand at the small of her back, knowing onlookers would interpret their actions as lovers seeking a moment for private conversation.

But that simple touch only served to remind him of what he'd touched the previous afternoon. Of the exquisite thrill of burying himself inside her heat. Of the way she gasped out her pleasure as he entered her.

He could think of about a hundred things he wanted to do with her right now. Enjoying a view of the harbor while being gawked at was at about a hundred and thirty-two. Talking about that damn photo was probably fifty slots lower.

What he should really be doing—finding a way to extricate himself from this relationship—was even lower than that. Of course, that was out the question now. Even he wasn't enough of an idiot to dump her under these circumstances.

But that did not explain why he'd rushed to her defense

by introducing himself as her fiancé. That was completely unexplainable. All he knew was that the second he'd seen Cynthia Rotham closing in for the kill, every protective instinct he had leaped to life. He'd spoken with no plan other than distracting Rotham.

Now that they were relatively alone, he said, "Neither of us could have anticipated this. What happened between us yesterday…" He stopped just shy of calling it a mistake. When he'd walked her to her car, she'd clearly been under the impression that sex up against the barn was going to lead to some kind of relationship. "Look, I should have stopped things before they got out of hand. I take full responsibility."

"*You* take full responsibility?" she sounded offended. "Why on earth would you be responsible for my actions? I'm an adult."

"Obviously. If you weren't, what happened yesterday would be illegal. Not to mention creepy." He flashed her a smile, hoping to lighten the mood. She didn't take the hint.

"I'm not joking." She stared him down with a hard gaze. All signs of the charmingly befuddled woman she'd been yesterday were now gone. "I don't blame you. It's not your mistake to take responsibility for."

"But I have more experience," he countered. "I should have—"

She tugged her arm from his grasp, still smiling cheerfully for anyone who might be watching as she said, "Yes, but I have more morals. If anyone should have stopped us, it's me."

The beginnings of a headache inched across his forehead. He rubbed his thumb across his brow to deaden the pain. "Morals aren't the issue here," he said under his breath.

"I just got caught—on film—mere minutes after having sex in public. With a stranger. I think morals are most definitely the issue."

"The picture looks worse than it was," he countered.

She glared at him from beneath her lashes. "We had sex up against the side of a barn. In full view of anyone who happened by." She threw up her hands as if pleading for mercy from some higher force. "The photo actually looks *better* than it was."

"True. But if they had a more incriminating picture, they would have used it. No one but us knows what actually happened."

The image of exactly what had happened between them played through his mind, unspooling in vivid and unforgettable detail. It was an effort, but he shut down his imagination. The last thing this conversation needed was him getting a hard-on. Or worse, coming on to her again.

Yeah, that would work great. *Hey, having sex with me just royally screwed up your life, but is there any chance you want to have another go at it?*

Unaware of his thoughts, she seemed to be considering his words, probably looking for the flaw in his logic. Finally, her shoulders seemed to relax. Only then did he realize how tensely she'd been holding herself. "Perhaps you're right. Maybe the photo they printed was the worst one they had." But she shook her head. "I still should have known better."

"You made one mistake."

The look she gave him was one of annoyance mingled with arrogance. "I didn't make just one mistake. I made the one mistake that could ruin my father's career."

"Don't you think that's overstating it a bit?"

"No. I don't. My actions reflect not just on me, but on him as well. The headline proved that." She shook her head, a faint glistening of tears in her eyes. "My mistake has stirred up all that old gossip about my mother. It's a disaster."

"Hey, whatever happened between your parents is their mistake, not yours. If your father blames you for that, then—"

She spun on him, her eyes alight with defensive fervor. "My father may not be the best father, but he's a great politician. He does amazing things for the good of this country. All he's ever asked of me is that I let him do his job. And now I've messed that up. Even if Cynthia Rotham bought your explanation, she's just one person. Everyone here has seen those pictures. Everyone who goes to that Web site will see those photos. For all I know, they're running the story on TMZ right this minute."

"What, you think I was just stepping in to defend you against Rotham?"

"I think you made a rash decision. You kept Cynthia from breathing down my neck. But she's far from the only one I'm worried about."

Before he could reply, her handbag buzzed loudly. She reached inside and pulled out her iPhone. "Great. A text from my father's senior staffer."

Grumbling under her breath, she stepped aside to respond.

The truth was, when he first spoke, he hadn't thought any further than the immediate crisis. He hadn't considered that the story might reach an audience broader than the gossips here in the Hamptons.

When she looked up, he said, "Okay. You're right. I didn't think this through. You'll have to excuse me. You're the first senator's daughter I've dated." At his use of the word "dated," she quirked an eyebrow. He ignored her silent commentary and pushed on. "I'm not used to life in the limelight. What do you suggest we do from here?"

She eyed him suspiciously. She held her phone in her hands, moving it between her thumb and forefinger like a string of rosary beads. After a moment, she shook her head. "I won't ask you to fix this for me."

"I don't leave my messes for other people to clean up."

She blanched as if he'd slapped her, and he instantly regretted his words.

"I am not your mess!" she snarled, turning on her heel and vanishing into the crowd.

So much for convincing the onlookers that they were blissfully engaged and planning a wedding.

She was right, of course. She wasn't his mess. She wasn't his anything. Nevertheless, he was to blame for this. He'd pursued her.

Knowing where she stood on the subject of casual sex, he'd pushed at her boundaries. He manipulated her into giving in to him. He'd created circumstances he'd known she wouldn't be able to resist.

And why had he done all of that? Because he was scared of how vulnerable she made him feel. Her own motives were so much purer. She talked about the good of the country and her father's career. Compared with her, he felt like a selfish jerk.

He prided himself on always getting what he went after. Now, that single-minded determination had gotten them both into serious trouble. And it was up to him to fix it.

Five

She didn't expect him to follow her.

If her behavior drove him to storm off, it would be a fitting end to her nightmare of a day. She made her way to the catering tent with the shortest line. One of the local Asian restaurants was offering up small takeout boxes brimming with stir-fried noodles and veggies. Brightly colored chopsticks stuck out of the boxes at an angle.

She snagged a box and a napkin, then made her way to one of the tables under a sprawling walnut. She stabbed the chopsticks into the box, digging around for a spear of broccoli. Pretending to eat without noticing the curious stares took all her concentration.

After a moment, Connor pulled out the chair beside her and sat down with his own box of noodles. Even without looking up, she felt his presence beside her.

Her emotions were still careening wildly out of control

and she couldn't muster the strength to offer the apology she knew he deserved.

"I never meant—" he began.

"I know." It was bad enough that she hadn't started with an apology. She couldn't sit here and listen to him apologize to her. She shifted to look at him. "You're right. This is a bad situation. Blaming one another certainly won't help. But I just can't ask you to sacrifice yourself for my mistake."

"*Our* mistake," he pointed out.

"No," she shook her head, "my mistake. You're the ladies' man. You're the charming smooth talker whom no woman can resist." His expression seemed to be hardening as she spoke, but she kept going. "I should have been stronger. I can't fault you for making me forget my standards. They're mine. If I don't stand by them, I have no one to blame but myself."

He tossed his chopsticks onto the table beside his takeout box, then leaned back in his chair. "So what you're saying," he spoke slowly and clearly, as if wanting to guarantee that she understood, "is that you don't blame me because I'm an amoral jerk. You, on the other hand, are to blame for even associating with me. And you should have known better."

"That is not what I said!"

He cocked his head to the side, his gaze steady and assessing. "Then what did you mean?"

"Just that—" But she broke off, because she couldn't think when he was watching her so closely. He muddled her mind. And she'd learned the hard way how easily he could trap her with his logic. "What I meant was, I knew what was at stake. True, I had no way of knowing we'd be caught, but I've lived my whole life in the public eye. I know better than most that every mistake you make comes back to haunt you. I should have known better."

His expression softened a little, as if her words were getting through to him. He ducked his head slightly, giving his expression a rueful puppy-dog quality. "True, you may have more experience with the press, but I have more experience with sex. I should have put a stop to things. I should have known they were getting out of hand. I just…"

He let his words trail off with a wry twist of a smile.

The implication hung there in the air between them. He hadn't stopped for the same reason she hadn't thought about the press. Their passion had gotten out of hand. Not because they were careless, but because this thing between them was more powerful than either of them expected.

In that instant, all of her doubts and self-recriminations vanished. She was back beside the barn, watching his expression as he looked at her near-naked body for the first time. Once again, she was flooded with that feeling of power, that sense that this passion between them was right. As if it was what she was born to do. As if her body had been created solely for the purpose of enticing him, just as his was made purely to bring her pleasure.

It was a heady feeling, this power she had over him, this passion that bloomed between them. It was stronger than anything she'd ever faced before. It was such a shame that she'd never get to experience it again.

He was a dangerous man. He'd already tempted her beyond anything she'd thought possible. She'd have to be even more careful around him.

He opened his mouth but she cut him off with a wave of her chopsticks. She didn't think she could stand any more confessions from him. "Let's just say we're both to blame and leave it at that."

He nodded, apparently willing to let that discussion go. "The question is, how do we fix it?"

"I don't know that we can."

"Trust me," he grinned. "I can fix this. I can fix any-thing."

He popped a bit of pork into his mouth. As he chewed, his smile held that touch of arrogance she found so exasperating. And yet somehow endearing, too. Gazing into his eyes, something caught inside her. She simultaneously wanted to cuddle against his chest and strip off her clothes. The urge to rest her head on his chest scared her more.

She forced herself to roll her eyes. "Fix it? Like your lie to Congresswoman Rotham? That didn't fix anything. Even if she believed you—"

"How much do you know about what I do?" he asked, cutting her off.

She stilled, a noodle midway to her mouth, surprised by the sudden shift in topic. "I know you're a hedge-fund manager, but I don't know more than that."

"Being a hedge-fund manager is a confidence game. I talk people into trusting me with huge amounts of money. For me to do that, they have to have absolute faith in me."

She could imagine. That smile of his alone—half self-deprecating, half charm—was pure confidence. If the job required him to win people over, he must be a natural at it. You just *wanted* to trust him.

Trusting him had created this problem. Falling for his charm had gotten her into this mess. Despite that, when he said, "Trust me," she wanted to.

"I came from nothing," he continued. "When I first started in this business, all I had was a good education, a hell of a lot of determination and my own belief I could succeed. On that alone, I convinced those first few people to hand over their fortunes. If I can do that, I can convince people that we're engaged."

She could imagine him charming people out of their money. Not because he intended to steal it out from under them but because he knew he could make them more, and he had the guts to go after his dream. She'd been subject to his persuasive tactics herself. She knew how convincing he could be.

Yet even now, she couldn't blame him for seducing her. No, his seduction had worked because he spoke to something inside of her, something no one else had tapped into. The experience had rocked her to her very soul. It shattered every belief she'd had about herself.

Which was precisely why she couldn't find it in her heart to wish she hadn't experienced it. Put simply, having sex with Connor was one of the best experiences of her entire life. Now that she'd had it, she couldn't wish it away any more than she could her own DNA. It was a part of her. Now she just had to learn to live with the repercussions.

Even if their fake engagement worked and her reputation stayed intact, she'd never again be the person she was before she met Connor Stone.

Connor couldn't read Brittney's emotions. She'd been silent while he spoke. Trying to gauge her reaction, his heart started pounding. What was up with that?

After all the clients he'd wooed, all the deals he'd put together, all the hundreds of millions of dollars he'd made— through all of that, he'd been as relaxed as a debutant getting her nails done. But *this* made him nervous?

All he could figure was for the first time, he actually cared about the gamble he was taking. With every other risk he'd taken, he'd always known something else was right around the corner. If he lost a client, he'd find another. If a deal fell through, he'd put together another one. If he lost money, he'd just make more. He never once doubted that he'd make it work one way or another. But with Brittney…well, there was only one of her. If he screwed this up, there'd be no second chance.

"What do you say? Do you trust me?" he prodded.

She searched his face, her eyes wide as she bit down on her lip. Finally she nodded. "I do."

All too aware of their surroundings, he set down his chopsticks and cupped her jaw with his palm. He ran his thumb across her cheek, entranced by how smooth her skin was. She blushed in response to his touch, her breath coming in a delicate tremble. The pink in her cheeks made her look unexpectedly vulnerable, and once again, the usually unflappable Brittney looked charmingly disheveled.

"Connor, really—"

He cut off her protest by kissing her. For an instant, she stiffened. Then, he ran his tongue along the seam of her lips, the gentlest of requests. Her mouth opened beneath his.

He deepened the kiss, his tongue moving against hers in a subtle imitation of the intimate act they'd performed just the day before. She lost herself in the kiss almost immediately, as if she'd been waiting all day for this moment, though she hadn't given him the slightest indication she had. Her hands clutched at his shoulders, and he felt her tension seep out of her.

His blood surged in response, but this time he didn't let his desire get the better of him. He kept one hand on her face, the other on her shoulder, focusing all his attention on just kissing her. Slowly, sensuously. Like a man content to spend all day doing only that.

And then, just as he'd planned, flashes went off. The paparazzi had arrived.

The burst of camera flashes snapped Brittney back to the present so quickly it made her head spin. One minute, Connor was kissing her with such soul-wrenching thoroughness she could barely remember her own name. The next she was the target of half a dozen flashing cameras.

Her mind reeled, only a single coherent thought tumbling through it: how the hell had this happened to her again?

She struggled to her feet, with Connor rising beside her. His hand was steady and sure at her back. He did not look nearly as surprised as she felt. Before she could wonder why, a reporter from one of the cable gossip shows shoved a microphone in her direction.

"This is the second time in two days you've been caught in a compromising position, Ms. Hannon. Would you care to comment?"

A second, less polite reporter pushed her microphone forward. "Any truth to the rumours about an engagement?"

"That 'good girl' comment must have really pissed you off, huh? Guess you have more of your mother in you than you've been letting on," a third reporter asked.

Brittney blinked as her confusion washed away in the wake of her anger. She was basically a peaceful person, but everyone had a breaking point. She reached out a hand, ready to grab the microphone and shove it somewhere creative.

Connor, it seemed, had not lost control of his faculties the way she had. He grabbed her hand and clutched it to his chest in a gesture that seemed cuddly rather than preventative. Then, to her amazement, he chuckled.

"You caught us again." He bumped his forehead against hers in show of playful affection. Then he turned the force of his charming smile on the reporters. "I just can't keep my hands off her. Can you blame me?"

She'd thought he'd worked a miracle with Cynthia Rotham, but that was nothing compared with how he handled the press. In the next fifteen minutes, he transformed the pack of microphone-wielding vicious paparazzi into a group about as bloodthirsty as papillon puppies.

By the time the reporters left, they were all smiling and chuckling. He'd convinced every one of them that she and

Connor were head over heels in love and—most importantly—that the photos from the day before were of innocent canoodling. Connor had one guy sharing tips on how to deal with meddling in-laws. Someone else had promised to e-mail him the name of a wedding caterer. She half expected Connor to toss them dog treats as they walked away.

Instead, he just smiled cheerfully and waved at them. Throughout the ordeal, he kept one arm firmly around her shoulder, glued to her as if he expected her to bolt.

Her own smile, she was sure, looked considerably less natural than his. "That was..." She shook her head. "I can't even think of words to describe what that was."

"Clever," he supplied easily. "Brilliant. Inspired."

She looked at him sideways. Dang it, but he was good-looking, with his easy smile and rakish black hair. "Do you always manage to get people to do exactly what you want?"

The look he gave her was surprisingly serious. "Only when it's really important."

"And this," she gestured to where the reporters had been. "Convincing these reporters that we're in love and that that photo yesterday was innocent—that's really important to you?"

As bizarre as it seemed, that was the only explanation that made sense.

"Is that so hard for you to believe?" he asked.

"Yes." She studied him again. She was used to his easy charm. It was the serious expressions she had trouble reading. "I just wonder what's in it for you."

He removed his arm from around her shoulder and shoved his hands deep in his pockets. "I clean up my messes."

And there it was again. The second time he'd referred to her as a mess. Something to be cleaned up and taken care of. Why was she destined to be people's mistakes? She'd known her whole life that her father saw her as an inconvenience at best, a political scandal waiting to re-erupt at worst. It was bad enough her own father saw her as a burden—she couldn't stand for Connor to see her that way, too.

She'd worked so hard to maintain her independence. She took care of herself. She never made mistakes, because it was the only way to guarantee that no one would ever have to rescue her.

Yet she was Connor's big mess. Once again a man she admired more than she wanted to saw her as little more than an inconvenience.

"We've gone over this already. It's my mess," she insisted. "Not yours."

"That's where you're wrong. If I hadn't been bent on seducing you, this never would have happened."

"Why? Because you're so irresistible?" As soon as she said the words, she regretted them. He *was* irresistible. Hadn't he proved that over and over again? Before he could answer, she snapped, "Get that smug expression off your face."

He shrugged innocently. "I didn't say anything."

"Yeah, but you were about to," she accused.

As if she needed to hear more on that subject. Yes, he was irresistible. Yes, every time he touched her she lost all sense of herself. Blah, blah, blah. Enough already.

This man had turned her life upside down in just a few days. A lifetime of perfect behavior, and she threw it out the window just because he's a good kisser? She'd had enough of this crap. She was taking control again. Starting now.

"Here's the deal." She rounded on him and poked a finger in his chest. "From here on out, I'm calling the shots."

He raised his eyebrows but said nothing.

True, so far, he'd handled things brilliantly. He was a genius at manipulating the press—as well as Cynthia Rotham. But she couldn't afford to let him manipulate her, as well. She was already far more drawn to him than was healthy. If they were going to spend the summer pretending to be in love, she'd have to find a way to put some emotional distance between them.

"If you really feel so bad about this," she said, "then you'll follow my lead and keep your mouth shut."

His lips quirked, as if the idea of following anyone's lead greatly amused him.

"Obviously you're good at handling the press, so you can be in charge of them. But when we're alone, I'm in charge. Do you think you can do that or not? Because if you can't—"

He pulled her to him and planted a firm kiss on her lips.

She wedged her hands against his chest and pushed, creating some room between them. "And no more kissing! And definitely no more sex! From here on out, it's strictly platonic."

"Of course," he agreed in a voice that didn't wholly convince her. It might have helped if he weren't still holding her body tightly to his.

"I mean it. We'll be engaged in public, but in private there'll be no canoodling, innocent or otherwise."

"And how long exactly am I supposed to live like a monk?"

She thought for a moment. "At least until the end of the polo season. After we return to the city, we'll be out of the spotlight and we can break things off."

She half expected him to protest. The end of the season was five weeks away.

But he just nodded. "Okay."

"Okay? You can really go that long—"

"Yes," he said, looking a little chagrined. "I can wait that long."

"Fine. Then you should start by letting me go."

"I would. But there's another reporter hiding behind the tent pole with his camera. It wouldn't do for us to be seen fighting in public."

She didn't have a chance to look over her shoulder and verify the reporter behind the pole, because the arrogant jerk leaned down and kissed her again.

Six

Just as they both hoped, the news about their relationship quickly overshadowed the gossip about the photo. Their engagement made the headlines and disappeared from the papers almost without her father's notice. There were several communications via his staff, but not so much as an e-mail from him personally. She was determined to view his lack of concern as faith in her ability to choose well.

After all, her father's interest in her love life had begun and ended with her brief stint dating Phillip. Their relationship had ended two years ago, and her father still met Phillip for golf every Saturday morning.

Given her tenuous relationship with her father, she was glad he didn't come out for the polo season anymore. She stayed at his house on Long Pond because she had enough flexibility in her schedule to work from home. Though she had the house and grounds to herself, she stayed in the guest quarters out by the pool, having converted one of the cottage's two bedrooms into an office. She spent her weekdays ensconced there, neck deep in Java code. Normally when she summered at her father's house, she got a tremendous amount of work done. But this year, her social calendar filled up faster than she could turn things down.

By lunch each Friday, Connor was back. The first two weekends, he'd stayed at a local hotel. But when she found out where he was staying, she insisted he take one of the bedrooms in her father's sprawling mansion.

"It's ten thousand square feet with no one in it except for the staff. My father never comes anymore, so there's no reason you shouldn't stay there," she told him the second Sunday of the polo season as they sat in the bleachers, watching a match.

"I can afford a hotel." His tone was terse—not unpleasant, but not the easy relaxed baritone she'd grown used to in such a short period of time.

She pulled her gaze from the match she was barely paying attention to and slanted a look at him. He was hard to read, his expression inscrutable. Charm came so easily to him, she hardly knew what to make of the tension she read in his shoulders or the curtness of his words.

She wanted to ask what was wrong. But that seemed like such a girlfriend thing to do. There could be a hundred things bothering him.

It could be work. She'd lived her whole life under the political microscope, but that was nothing compared with juggling billions of dollars in investments.

It could be something with his family. From comments he'd made, she gathered he had a large extended family, most of whom he wasn't close to but still kept in touch with. Her own family tree was tall but narrow. Only her grandmother, father and she remained from a line that stretched all the way back to the Pilgrims. Yet sometimes keeping just her father and grandmother happy was difficult enough. She couldn't imagine trying to negotiate the needs of three siblings, plus parents, aunts, uncles, cousins, etc. Surely that would be reason enough for him to be tense.

And of course, she realized with a thudding heart, it could be someone else. After all, what did she really know about his personal life, or about him? Yes, he'd come on to her, quite persuasively and persistently. But that didn't mean he didn't have someone else in the wings.

Before she could stop herself, she asked, "Is it someone else?"

"What?"

His baffled look made her instantly regret her question.

She forced her gaze back to the polo field where the horses and black-clad riders of the Black Wolves zipped by in a blur. "You seemed upset. I thought maybe…" She let her words trail off, unsure how to phrase the question that now seemed both presumptuous and ridiculous.

But he wouldn't let her get away with it. "You thought what?"

"I don't know, that maybe there was someone back in New York who was unhappy about this…" Again she trailed off, unable to put into words the complicated tangle of lies they'd fallen into.

"Someone like a girlfriend?"

If she'd thought his tone was tense before, it was nothing compared with the blunt force of his words now.

"Yes," she admitted defensively. "Like a girlfriend."

"You thought I had a girlfriend. In New York. That I didn't bother to mention."

"It didn't seem impossible," she hedged. Other men had done that kind of thing before. Phillip, for example.

"You don't think it would have come up before now?"

"Well, it's not like our engagement was something we had time to plan."

"True," he drew the word out. "But it was something I came up with. I wouldn't have suggested it if I had girlfriend in the city." Then he shook his head as if unable to believe he was even having this conversation. "Hell, if I had a girlfriend in the city, I wouldn't have slept with you in the first place. What kind of guy do you think I am?"

She tried not to cringe. "Look, I'm sorry. Obviously I offended—"

"Damn straight you offended me."

"You wouldn't be the first guy in the world to cheat and get caught."

"No, but I also wouldn't be the first guy in the world to make a mistake and do the honorable thing."

Good point. One she wished she'd thought of before opening her mouth.

He sat forward, ostensibly to watch the action at the far end of the field. But she couldn't help noticing the movement angled his back toward her. His shoulders, even tenser than before, were like a wall of unspoken accusations between them.

All she could do now was apologize. "I guess I don't know that many honorable guys." She raised her hand to hover just above his shoulder. "I'm sorry."

Her hand hung there for a moment in awkward indecision before she lowered it to his back. The muscles of his shoulder jumped under her hand, solid and unyielding. Instantly she wished she hadn't touched him. Then he straightened. He took her hand and wove his fingers through hers.

"Stop comparing me with other men you've known."

His hand was warm against hers, reassuring somehow, his gaze steady and confident. There was nothing sexual about the way he looked at her, but still, she felt a shiver of something heated and dark go through her.

Yes, she should definitely stop comparing him with other

men. The other men would always come up short. And she had the uncanny sensation that would always be true. That for the rest of her life, no man she ever met would measure up.

One summer with Connor Stone had ruined her for other men.

Brittney's delicate hand felt good in his. And for an instant, he nearly forgot that he didn't really have the right to hold it. If they weren't in public, she might not even allow him to touch her.

He took comfort in the fact that she'd obviously forgotten, too. Her expression shifted from one of doubt to delightfully befuddled confusion. She looked slightly shell-shocked. Well, good. He liked her off balance, and he thought it probably did her a world of good to have someone in her life who didn't do exactly what she expected.

She half-heartedly attempted to pull her hand from his, but he didn't let go, and she quickly gave in. Whether because her resistance was weak or because she didn't want to cause a scene, he didn't know.

It only bothered him a little that he didn't *want* to know. That he wanted to pretend it was because she wanted to hold his hand. To distract them both, he asked, "What brought this on anyway?"

"You seem tense," she answered after a minute. "Angry, almost. I thought maybe you were mad about having to keep up the facade for so long."

"I knew what I was getting into when I agreed to this."

She was certainly perceptive. Which wasn't surprising, given her experience in politics. He'd always thought of himself as being good at hiding his emotions. But you probably had to be pretty good at reading people to work on a political campaign.

"If you don't want to tell me what's wrong, it's fine," she said.

But her hand had tensed in his and he knew it wasn't really fine. Saying nothing would widen the gap between them.

He wasn't the kind of guy who opened up and shared his feelings very often—bonding just wasn't his thing. Maybe it was his solidly stoic, middle-American background. To his way of thinking, if you couldn't say it with a sports analogy or show it with car care, it wasn't worth saying. But as far as he knew, Brittney had a full-time driver in the city who took damn good care of her car and she didn't watch football.

He stared at the polo players galloping across the field, their horses gleaming and massive, their movements a ballet of aggressive grace, their strikes at the ball borderline violent. Yet the sport oozed elegance. Wealth and privilege. It was a world he worked and flirted with. But it wasn't the world he was born to. He'd been reminded of that spending these last few weeks with Brittney.

His blue-collar upbringing didn't bother him. But apparently it bothered her. Why else would she balk at introducing him to her father, the senator? And that *did* bother him. He didn't care what ninety-nine percent of the world thought of him. But her opinion mattered.

How the hell could he put that into words?

He tried. "I'm football and you're polo."

"You don't like watching polo?" She frowned, her forehead furrowing in that cute, confused way. "If you don't like it, you don't have to come out for every match."

"No. That's not it. It's a great sport. But I didn't grow up watching it. I was probably twenty before I knew it was sport, not just a logo on T-shirts."

"Oh," she nodded in understanding. Then she leaned forward. "Okay, look at that player on the sorrel pony. That horse is Maximo. He's ridden by Nicolas Valera. He's—"

He laughed, cutting her off. "No, I get the sport. I understand what they're doing."

"Then what's the problem?" Again she was frowning.

Man, she did not let things go.

"We're from different worlds. And it shouldn't be an issue. But—" He rolled his shoulders trying to release some of the tension that had taken up residence there. When had this gotten so complicated? "Look, I know why you'd be hesitant, but people will start wondering what's going on if I don't at least meet your father."

She twisted sharply in her seat to stare at him. "What? Meet my...what are you talking about?"

"Your father? The senator? The guy whose house you invited me to stay in because there's no way he'll come out to the Hamptons this season? That guy. That ring any bells for you?"

After another moment of doe-eyed gaping during which he wondered if he would have to spell it out for her more clearly, she grinned.

"That's what this is about? You think I'm embarrassed of you?"

He turned his attention back to the polo field. "I didn't say that."

"Oh, no. You didn't, did you?" She laughed. "Sheesh. Men." She faked a deep voice. "I'm football, you're polo. I don't have conversations about my feelings, so I'll just use a sports analogy. Maybe if I go long, she'll be able to hit a home run."

He wanted to be annoyed by her teasing. Really he did— and, damn it, how did she see right through him?—but he couldn't resist chuckling at her fumbled analogy. "Are you talking about football or baseball?"

"You know, you haven't exactly invited me to meet your family, either."

"Good point." He nodded. "Any time you want to experience the torture of driving out to Pennsylvania so my mom can throw a barbecue and introduce you to my brothers, their families, a dozen aunts and uncles and probably thirty or so cousins—plus neighbors—you just tell me and I'll set that up."

She looked baffled, like she'd been doing his family math in her head and had crossed over into the triple digits. "I…"

"I'm joking. I already called my mom and told her the truth. Don't worry, I swore her to secrecy and she'd drink hemlock before betraying the trust of one of her kids."

"I'm not worried," she reassured him.

"I didn't want her to get too excited. She generally ignores social gossip, but she salivates at the thought of grandchildren."

"Oh." Her tone sounded almost wistful. "No, I don't need to meet your family. But they sound nice."

He did a double take. "Nice? Crazy and overwhelming is how they sound." He studied her face, taking in the way her attempt at a smile didn't quite reach her eyes. "Why? What did your father say?"

"Oh, all the normal things you'd expect. He couldn't wait to welcome you to the family personally. He's impressed by you and thinks you're a shining example of how hard work and education can help the ambitious rise above their humble beginnings." Her lips twisted into a wry smile. "Didn't you watch his press conference?"

"Actually, I did. My secretary sent me the link on Hulu." He noticed that Brittney hadn't mentioned anything her father hadn't covered in the press conference. "You did actually talk to your father, didn't you?"

Brittney didn't meet his gaze but stared out at the polo field as if engrossed. "He's been very busy."

Connor did a quick scan of the field. Nope, none of the

players had sprouted wings. "You just got engaged. Didn't he call to ask a few questions? Doesn't he want to know anything about me, the man who is supposed to marry his little girl?"

"I've talked to his senior staffer a lot. Of course we talk almost every day anyway. She forwarded me your file."

"My file?" he asked.

She cringed. "You probably don't want to know more than that. I don't ask where he gets his information. Sorry." She softened the news with a rueful smile. "If it makes you feel any better, there was a Post-It note with the words, 'Seems like a good choice' on it."

"Yeah. That's much better."

"I'm sorry about the file thing. I probably shouldn't have mentioned it."

"Forget it," he said gently, taking her hand again.

What was *she* apologizing for? Her father was total jerk and *she* was sorry?

He felt like he was the one who should apologize. His family actually cared about him. Her father couldn't find the time to pick up the phone and call. What an idiot.

Connor gave her hand a squeeze. "Does he know what a great daughter he has?"

"I'm a valuable asset to his political team. I hear that all the time." But did she hear it from her father or from his staff? And did it matter? Being a valuable asset was not the same thing as being loved.

He was about to comment on exactly that when she changed the subject. "So, will you come stay at my father's place? I know money isn't an object for you—" she held up a hand as if to ward off his protests "—but I'd feel better knowing you're not in a hotel room every weekend. Besides, I live in the guest cottage so the main house is empty. Surely you'd be more comfortable having a place of your own instead of hauling things back and forth. And—"

She broke off, seeming hesitant.

"What is it?" he asked.

"Zoe, dad's staffer, has been talking about wanting him to throw us an engagement party at the end of the season. But don't worry. I'll convince her to call it off."

"Don't." Connor had trouble keeping his dislike from his voice, but he tried, for her. "Let your dad do his worst. It's only money, right? Just don't let him serve those little wieners on sticks. Make him pay for fancy appetizers."

She grinned. "Okay. I'll let Zoe know."

"I will come stay at the house. If it'll make you feel better."

"It will," she reassured him. "This whole thing has been enough of a mess as it is. I hate the thought of being even more of an inconvenience to you."

She made the comment in an offhand manner, turning her attention to the playing field as she said it. This time she really was watching the game, relaxing into the match.

Yet her words stuck with him. He could read between the lines. Because of the circumstances of her birth, she had been inconvenient to Senator Hannon's career. But instead of finding a way to look past that, it had affected his relationship with his daughter. Instead of seeing Brittney for the bright and wonderful woman she was, he saw her as a burden, despite the fact that she'd lived her whole life seeking his approval. By her own admission, she'd done a little boundary pushing in high school. But apparently she'd quickly realized that the affections of high school boys didn't make up for a father's love—thank God for that. Some women never made that intellectual leap. Since then, she'd been a model daughter. Every decision—personal and professional—had benefited her father's career. And the man was too much of a jerk to see it or appreciate it.

In that moment, Connor hoped he never did meet Senator Hannon. He just might punch the man.

He didn't think of himself as a violent person, but here he was, ready to coldcock someone for hurting Brittney. Again. First he'd been ready to trample some reporter, and now her father.

Where had these protective instincts come from? And what was it about her that stirred them up so easily?

Seven

The few remaining weeks of the polo season passed in a blur of social events. Even though she'd spent every summer in the Hamptons since she was a child, she'd never before been so busy. Connor was by her side the whole time, but she was rarely alone with him. And though he flirted outrageously with her, he never again pressed her to revisit the physical side of their relationship. But she knew she was in trouble. She was starting to fall for him. Her only consolation was in knowing that the summer would soon be over and her life would return to normal.

Before she knew it, the date of her engagement party had arrived. Decorators and caterers hired by her father's staff descended on the house three days before the party. During what would be the last few days of their relationship, she barely saw Connor at all. Which was probably for the best. What could come of it? Either she'd break down and beg him to make love to her one last time, or she'd do something really stupid like tell him she was falling in love with him.

On the night of the party, Brittney moved through the crowd with practiced ease. A lifetime of experience pretending to be the perfect senator's daughter was serving her well. No one watching her would sense how conflicted she felt.

From the first awkward introduction to her father and onward, Connor was by her side throughout the first part of the evening. If Connor felt any apprehension about meeting him, he didn't show it. His presence alleviated the strain between her and her father, those quiet, clumsy moments when neither of them knew what to say to the other. Connor's hand was warm and strong at her back.

And once her father left to talk to people he thought more important, Connor stayed by her side as she chatted with other guests, his charm smoothing over awkward silences, his wit providing answers to questions she couldn't anticipate.

Under other circumstances, she might have been unnerved by how easily he lied, but for now she was just grateful.

"Where did you meet?" people inevitably asked.

"Standing in line, waiting to pick up takeout at Brit's favourite Thai place. What's the name of the place, honey?"

"Topaz Thai," she'd mumble awkwardly.

"How long have you been together?" other people prodded.

"Almost three months now," he lied smoothly. "At first it was tough keeping our relationship secret. But I didn't want Brit to worry about the stress of dating in the public eye. So we managed it." Then he smiled ruefully, giving her shoulder a subtle squeeze. "Until we got caught."

Eventually, someone was bold enough to look pointedly at the bare ring finger of her left hand. "I do hope you're not going to be one of those modern couples who don't bother to have a ceremony in a church or even wear rings."

Connor just smiled at the nosy old biddy who made that comment. "No, ma'am," he said. "I'm having a ring made. I wanted Brit to wear my grandmother's ring. But I'm from a simple, working-class family. I knew Brit would love any ring I gave her, but I wanted her to be proud to wear it." He gave her shoulder a squeeze for effect. "So I'm having a small diamond and lapis stones taken out and replaced with a larger diamond and sapphires."

By the time he finished describing the ring, the old lady had tears in her eyes. She wasn't the only one. Brittney had to excuse herself before she welled up like an idiot.

Alone, with her back propped against the bathroom door, she wiped furiously at her tears. Why was she crying over a ring she wasn't ever going to get? The ring wasn't real. It was just a story meant to placate curious busybodies. That guy who had carefully designed and crafted that ring to give to his fiancée? He wasn't any more real than the ring.

Oh, but more and more she wished he were. She wished Connor were not just handsome and charming, but sincere as well. What would it be like to be loved by that man, and not just seduced by the playboy?

Connor was probably the first fiancé in the history of the world to hope for a if-you-hurt-my-little-girl-I'll-kill-you speech. When Senator Hannon angled to talk to Connor alone for a few minutes midway through the party, Connor actually hoped that's what he was in for. Until now, the senator had been blasé about their engagement. Connor knew her father's disinterest hurt Brittney's feelings. Why couldn't the guy at least feign concern?

But when the senator lead Connor from the party to the relative quiet of his study, Connor quickly realized that this meeting wasn't going to involve any protective speeches.

Senator Hannon poured Connor a Scotch and handed it

over, saying, "As you've probably realized, my daughter can be a bit strong-willed."

Connor said nothing but clenched the tumbler of Scotch in his hand. The senator's asinine opinions weren't Connor's problem to deal with. In a few short days, they'd be back in the city. A few weeks after that, as he and Brittney had agreed, they'd quietly end their engagement. He'd never have to see Senator Hannon again.

The fact that he'd never see Brittney again either was a matter he'd been studiously not thinking about.

"I suppose," the senator continued as he sat down behind the desk, "her intentions are good enough, but she has a tendency get the press riled up." He chuckled. "As I'm sure you've seen."

Connor nodded noncommittally, resisting the urge to point out that if it hadn't been for the senator's own indiscretions years ago, no one would care what Brittney did.

The senator cleared his throat. "The point is, it's an election year and I'd appreciate it if you would do what you can to keep her from making any more social gaffes in the next couple of months."

Connor was torn between wanting to laugh at the irony and wanting to beat the guy to a pulp. He settled for plunking the untouched glass of Scotch down on the senator's desk, propping his hands on the blotter and leaning forward.

"With all due respect, Senator, you're an idiot. If you cared half as much about your daughter as she does about your career, you'd be a better man. But since you don't, let me tell you a few things about her. She would never consciously do anything to hurt your career." He leaned ever closer, so the senator had to rock back in his chair. "And when we're married, I'd appreciate it if you'd do what you can to stay out of our lives."

And with that, Connor turned and walked away, leaving

the senator alone in stunned silence. It wasn't until he was back in the bustle of the party that he realized what he'd done. He'd spoken to Brittney's father as if they really were getting married. For a few minutes, he'd completely forgotten that their relationship was a lie. And that their ruse was about to come to an end.

After hours of mingling, smiling and bearing the painful congratulations of strangers, Brittney grabbed a glass of wine and found a quiet corner of the patio where she could recuperate.

She spotted Vanessa and Nicolas sneaking back toward the party from the formal gardens. There were spots throughout the gardens where an amorous couple could seize a few moments alone. It looked as though maybe Vanessa and Nicolas had done just that. Brittney had suspected they might be involved again several weeks ago, but his recent declaration at the polo match left no one in doubt of their relationship. The normally cool and reserved Nicolas had ridden up to Vanessa on his favorite horse, Maximo, and announced before God and everyone that he loved her. The act was all the more romantic because he was normally so cool and reserved. His grand gesture had melted the heart of every female there.

Until that moment, Brittney had doubted that the vivacious Vanessa could find happiness with such a man, but his actions that day had removed all of Brittney's doubts. And Vanessa's too, it seemed.

Brittney was thrilled for Vanessa's obvious contentment. But a little jealous, as well. It seemed as though everyone was destined to find love this summer, except Brittney.

Though, if she were honest with herself, that was not entirely true. She had found love. It just hadn't found her.

As Vanessa and Nicolas approached her hiding place, they paused. Nicolas bent down as Vanessa rose onto her toes.

At first Brittney feared she'd caught them about to kiss. But after a moment, she realized they were whispering. Nicolas reached up to twirl a lock of Vanessa's hair around his finger. Somehow the gesture was even more intimate than a kiss would have been.

Her cheeks burning, Brittney turned away and crept back to the house. They were too involved in one another to notice.

She snuck back into the party, painfully aware of her heated cheeks and thundering heart. The intimacy between Vanessa and Nicolas had unnerved her. It was true intimacy, of spirit and heart, not just body. The whispered moment between them was packed with more emotion than any passionate embrace.

Pressing the back of her hand to her cheek, she scanned the perimeter of the room for a tray where she could drop her empty glass. She barely noticed the man in front of her before she nearly walked into him.

"Hey, if it isn't the lucky lady herself." The man gave her arm a jovial, "'atta-girl" slap.

Try as she might, she couldn't suppress her cringe. He didn't notice anyway. Giving her arm a quick rub to take the sting out, she appraised him. Mid-thirties, manufactured smile, designer suit, hair meticulously styled to disguise the fact that it was thinning. He looked familiar, but if she had to guess, it was because he looked like half the men in New York, not because she actually knew him.

"Excuse me for asking, but have we met?" she asked as politely as she could.

"No," he slurred. "But I know you. In fact, I take credit for all of this." He waved a hand at the party taking place.

"Oh, then you must be John from the catering company." She extended her hand.

As the man shook her hand, he leaned in close. "No, I'm not a caterer." He laughed like the idea was hysterical. Then, still holding her hand, he winked and gave her a little toast with his glass. "For you and Connor."

"I'm sorry." She tugged at her hand, trying to get him to release it. "I don't understand."

"That night at the bar. You two never would have met if I hadn't bet Connor he couldn't get you into bed."

Connor watched from across a sea of people as Tim struck up a conversation with Brittney. Even from this distance, he could tell Tim had been drinking too much. Tim always got chummy when he was soused, slapping people on the arm and laughing with glee. His mouth sometimes got him into trouble when he was sober. Put a couple of drinks in him, and it was a disaster.

This was not a guy Connor wanted talking to Brittney.

He quickly excused himself from the conversation on trade restrictions he'd gotten suckered into with a colleague of Brittney's father. As he wended his way through the crowd, he kept an eye on her. Her expression drifted from confused to offended. She had the grace and good breeding to hide her feelings generally—Tim must have said something bad for offense to register on her face.

Connor picked up the pace as he elbowed past a giggling socialite. He walked up behind Brittney just in time to hear Tim saying, "You two never would have met if I hadn't bet Connor he couldn't get you into bed."

Before Tim even finished the sentence, Connor put his hand on Brittney's back. She flinched at his touch, jerking back to look up him. Her brow was furrowed as she looked from Connor to Tim and back again.

"Is he…" she began, but seemed unable to finish the sentence.

Connor managed a smile and said, "Tim, what kind of lies are you telling my fiancée about me?"

He reached out to shake Tim's hand in greeting while keeping his other hand firmly and possessively on Brittney's back, hoping that she'd read his sincerity in his touch.

"No, man," Tim said, giving Connor's hand an overly firm shake. "No lies. That was what, six or seven weeks ago, right? We were all at that jazz bar. You hit on Brittney."

Tim's voice started to rise with his insistence, and people nearby were turning to look as they couldn't help but overhear his drunken words. Connor could feel the tension growing in Brittney. Under his hand, her muscles had turned to rock and her posture was stick straight.

"She shot you down," Tim continued. "I tried to tell you she was out of your league, but you were determined to try again. Remember? I told you about the profile in that magazine. What's the name of that thing? The Profiler or something, right? That's when you bet me you'd get her into bed before the end of summer."

Tim paused to smile lewdly at Brittney. "So see, if it weren't for me, you two never would have gotten engaged." Tim gave Connor a whack on the arm. "Who knew this hound dog would ever settle down. Am I right?"

Connor forced another smile. "You're mistaken, buddy," he said to Tim in a voice just loud enough for others to overhear. He pulled Brittney tight against his side and dropped a kiss onto her forehead. "Six weeks ago, Brittney and I had already been dating for a couple of months. But we were still keeping our relationship a secret. I pretended to hit on her to have an excuse to say hello." Connor looked down at Brittney. Her expression was fixed, like she was trying to process too much information too quickly. "Isn't that right, honey?"

He gave her arm another squeeze, and after a second she nodded and smiled like the experienced navigator of social gaffes that she was. "Absolutely."

Tim looked first at Connor and then at Brittney. He was far

too slow to keep up. He looked like he wanted to argue, but Connor didn't give him a chance. Instead he gently steered the conversation around to Tim's work before making their excuses and maneuvering Brittney away.

Connor may have talked his way around Tim's confusion, but Brittney wouldn't be nearly so easy to manage. He could practically hear her thinking, figuring her way through the nonsense of Tim's rambling to the truth of that fateful conversation back at the beginning of the summer.

You wouldn't know it to look at her, though. As they moved through the crowd, she smiled with the ease that seemed second nature to her. And that made Connor very nervous.

She had the ability to conceal her distress so thoroughly that you could barely see any sign of it. But it was the defense mechanism she used when she was the most upset.

He'd rarely seen her this poised and smooth.

When he spotted the door to the butler's pantry, he steered her toward it. He didn't want her to have time to let Tim's words sink in and simmer.

The second the door closed behind them and they were alone, she shrugged off his touch.

"Brittney—" he began, but she held up a hand warding off his entreaty.

The butler's pantry was a long and narrow room connecting the main room to the kitchen. Glass-front cabinets lined both walls. Bottles of wine and empty glasses littered the soapstone countertops. Obviously the staff had been using the butler's pantry for its intended purpose, as a staging ground for the waiters distributing drinks and appetizers to the crowd. Which meant he wouldn't have long to explain before they were interrupted. He'd have to talk fast.

"I don't want to hear any more lies." She shivered, as if she was shedding something unpleasant. When she turned to face him, she had her arms wrapped around her waist.

"It's not how Tim made it sound."

"What, it's not like you saw me in a bar and decided to pick me up? It's not like you followed me out to the Hamptons to seduce me?" Her voice was tinged with bitterness. "Because, actually, it is like that. And I even knew it."

"Brittney," he reached a hand out to her, but even in the tight quarters, she managed to dodge his touch. "Tim made it sound like it was all just a bet. It wasn't."

"Yeah, well, it wasn't like you made it sound either. Like he was the ignorant rube in our little lover's game." She rolled her eyes. "God, you're so good at that."

"At what?"

"At making people believe what you want them to." Finally she met his gaze. "That's what makes you so dangerous."

The resolve he saw in her eyes sent a splash of icy dread over him. "You can't let what Tim said upset you. He's drunk and, well, kind of an idiot under the best of circumstances. And he's not remembering the way things really happened."

She let loose a bark of laughter. "Whatever gaps there may be in his memory, I can guarantee his version of that night is closer to the truth than the lies you just spun. That charming story about how we were keeping our relationship a secret? The way you only pretended to hit on me just to say hello?" She nodded in mock appreciation. "That's good stuff. Let's be sure to save that story for our grandchildren."

"Brittney—"

"Oh, wait. We're not going to have grandchildren. Because we're not really engaged. Nor are we really in love."

Connor heard a waiter reaching for the door behind him. With one hand, he grabbed the doorknob, holding the door shut. He reached for her again and caught her hand in his. Her fingers felt unnaturally cold, as if she were going into shock.

"Let's talk about this," he said. "Let me explain."

"What is there to explain? I know what happened. Don't get me wrong, I like the fairy tale, but I don't believe in it."

She gave her hand a tug, but he wouldn't let her go. Behind him, he could feel the waiter on the other side of the door struggling, but Connor kept his hand firmly on the knob, unwilling to have their conversation interrupted.

"You're upset. I'm not letting you leave like this."

She met his gaze again, slowly shaking her head. "It's okay. Really, it is." Again she tugged on her hand. Again he didn't loosen his hold on her. "The thing is, Connor, I—" Her voice broke and she swallowed back tears before continuing. "I think I really was starting to fall in love with you. I'd gotten so caught up in playing the role, I forgot it wasn't real. But the truth is, I hardly know you. All I know is this fantasy you've created, this persona of the perfect fiancé you've been playing for the past six weeks. Tim didn't tell me anything I didn't know. He just reminded me of reality."

Her gaze was so raw and pained, Connor could hardly stand to look her in the eyes. But he made himself. He'd done this to her. As proud as she was, as strong, as resilient—after all the things he'd done to try to protect her this summer—here he was, the one to break her.

"I know we agreed to break things off once we returned to the city, but I don't think I can wait that long. I can't pretend anymore. And I don't want to risk forgetting again."

Behind him, the waiter called out, "Hey, is there someone in there? I don't think anyone's supposed to be back there."

"Give us a minute," Connor ordered.

"No, it's okay," Brittney said quietly. "We're done here."

The waiter gave the knob one last violent turn, wrenching the door open. Brittney pulled her hand free and left through the door on the far side of the pantry.

She'd slipped right through his fingers.

Eight

Brittney received an unprecedented number of calls and e-mails during the days following her return to the city. Most were from people she hadn't had a chance to talk to during the party, wishing her congratulations. Some were from people who had noticed her early disappearance and who wanted to make sure she was all right—or to cash in on the gossip if she wasn't. A few were from people who seemed to be genuinely concerned. The only call she returned was Vanessa's. But she didn't have the heart to tell her friend what had happened, finding she couldn't put into words how quickly her well-ordered life had fallen apart.

The one person whom she hoped might call was Connor. For six weeks he'd been constantly by her side, defending her any time someone so much as spoke to her in a suggestive tone. But now, when she could use a shoulder to cry on, he was gone. Of course, he couldn't protect her from himself.

She stayed at home, working long hours on her father's Web

site, catching up on the work that hadn't gotten done over the summer. Almost an entire week went by without her seeing anyone other than the delivery guy from Topaz Thai. Finally, the Monday after she returned to the city, Vanessa came by and dragged her out for a lunch. While it was good to be in the company of another person, she hated how careful Vanessa seemed.

Brittney never thought of herself as a frail person. She didn't need coddling. Maybe it was being in the company of Vanessa—or maybe she simply felt more vulnerable than normal—but she found herself opening up and telling her the truth.

The two women sat across from each other in a little café just down the street from Brittney's condo, drinking coffee. Brittney poked morosely at the bright pink topping of her raspberry yogurt parfait.

"I should look on the bright side," she finally said. "I only fell a little bit in love with him."

Brittney nibbled on the tip of the spoon. She looked across the table at Vanessa only when she realized Vanessa had said nothing in response. She had an odd expression on her face—half wince, half cringe.

"What?" Brittney asked.

"Nothing," Vanessa said too quickly.

"No, it's not nothing. You looked like you wanted to say something."

"It's just—" Vanessa set down her spoon and leaned forward "—I don't think you can fall only a little bit in love."

"Of course you can fall only a little bit in love. My roommate in college did it all the time."

"Yes, of course *people* can. I meant I'm not sure *you* can."

"What are you saying? You think I'm defective?"

"No." Vanessa patted Brittney on the back of the hand. "I

just think maybe you're an all-or-nothing kind of girl." Then she paused and tilted her head to the side, considering. "What you said, about Connor doing all of this just because he felt guilty about that stupid bet? I don't buy it."

"Vanessa, he—"

"Because I swear, the way he looks at you sometimes, it reminds me of…" Vanessa shook her head, her expression pensive.

"Of what?"

"Well, of the way Nicolas looks at me."

Brittney nearly snorted with disbelief. "I've seen the way Nicolas looks at you. It's steamy, with intense possessiveness."

"Exactly!" Vanessa pointed her spoon at Brittney emphatically.

"I think new love is coloring your perspective. What you're imagining is love on Connor's part is merely…I don't know, indigestion or something." She smiled at the look on Vanessa's face. "But thank you for imagining he could be in love with me. You're a good friend."

Vanessa gave Brittney a wink. "I am, aren't I?"

Brittney couldn't help but laugh. She left their lunch feeling better.

On her way home, she thought about what Vanessa had said about her not being able to fall in love only a little bit. What if Vanessa were right? What if she'd fallen in love with a man who could never love her back? Being with Connor had unleashed a passionate side she'd always kept under tight control. What would happen to that part of her now that Connor wasn't in her life? Would she ever find another man with whom she felt so comfortable? And who stirred her emotions and her senses?

Later that night, she was contemplating that very depressing possibility while she waited for her takeout to be delivered.

Her bell rang and she buzzed the delivery guy in, ready for another night of Topaz Thai. But when she opened her door, she didn't find a guy with coconut soup.

Instead, she found Connor.

His appearance startled her. He'd never been less than impeccably dressed, even when dressed casually for the matches. Today he wore faded jeans and a plain white oxford shirt left untucked. He stood with his shoulder propped against the wall and his hands shoved deep into his pockets. His hair was messy, his face lined with exhaustion. He looked as if he hadn't slept in a week. In short, he looked as exhausted as she felt.

He didn't greet her, pushing his way into her apartment before she could protest. "I'm not giving you up," he announced.

She blinked. "You're what?"

"Not giving you up." With each word, he stalked a step closer to her. It wasn't long before he'd closed the distance between them. He wrapped a hand around her upper arm, keeping her from retreating. "I know this started out as just a ruse, but we're good together." His thumb circled the skin on the inside of her arm.

He did that kind of thing all the time, touching her so casually. It drove her to distraction, and she'd always assumed that was his intention. Now, watching him, she wondered if perhaps instead of a calculated enticement, the habit was more of a compulsion, as if he couldn't keep his hands off her, just as he'd told the reporters.

The idea that he might simply need to touch her was a tempting one. Too tempting. She couldn't let herself fall into that trap.

Pulling her arm away from his touch, she put some distance between them. "I'm sorry, Connor. I don't care how good we are in bed. I can't base a relationship on a single sexual experience. Sure, we could draw out this fake engagement for another six months or a year, but eventually, this will end. And no matter how or when that happens, it's going to be bad for me. At least if I end it now, I have some hope of getting over you."

He studied her features, his expression intense. Serious, in a way she'd never seen before. "What if it doesn't end? What if I don't want you to get over me?"

Her breath caught in her chest. "What are saying?"

"We make it real. We stay together. We make it work."

She backed up a step, sinking onto her sofa when it bumped against her legs. Her heart pounded as she considered his proposal.

That's what it was—a proposal. Probably the least romantic proposal she'd ever heard, but a proposal nevertheless. Funny, the complete lack of artifice almost won her over. Normally he was so smooth, so charming. Did this bare-bones proposal stem from genuine emotion?

And then she remembered what the last six weeks had been like. Watching him charm everyone he came in contact with. Listening to him tell lies so smoothly. Never knowing which Connor was the real Connor. Could she live like that for the rest of her life?

Shaking her head, she said, "No. I can't do it. Vanessa told me she thought I was an all-or-nothing kind of girl. That once I fell in love, it would be forever. I think she's probably right. I don't want to be in love with you forever."

He flinched as if she'd hauled back and punched him in the gut. Then, in an instant, his expression settled into quiet resolve, his jaw clenched. He turned to leave. "Okay."

If she hadn't been watching so closely, she would have missed the flash of pain completely. But she had seen it on his face, and she couldn't let him go without explaining.

She leaped to her feet and grabbed his arm before he made it to the door. "Let me explain."

He studied her, his expression cold and distant. "You were very succinct. No explanation is necessary."

"Connor, it's not that I don't *want* to love you. It's that I'm afraid to." She searched his face for understanding. When she didn't see any, she kept talking. "I've watched you this summer. You're a total chameleon, capable of being anything to anybody. I'd never know how you really felt about me."

"That's all?" he asked. "You're afraid I don't love you?"

She pulled her hand away. "Trust me. That's enough. I've spent my whole life never knowing whether or not my father loves me or if I was just a mistake he had to twist to his political advantage. I don't think I could stand not knowing if you—"

He wrapped his arms around her and cut off her explanation with a kiss. It was a breath-stealing, soul-searing kiss she felt down to her very bones, like he was pouring a lifetime's worth of reassurances into that one gesture.

When he pulled back, he said, "If you want to know how I feel about you, all you have to do is ask. You make me crazy. You terrify me. You make me do things I never thought I'd do."

"Is this bad or good?" she asked hesitantly.

"Good." He laughed an all-out laugh. "I've never felt this way about anyone else. There's no one else who knows me the way you do. And I have never lied to you."

"The bet—"

"Forget the bet. It was never about that for me. I would have pursued you hard, no matter what. Do you want to know why?"

She could only nod.

"I knew from the minute I met you that I was in serious trouble. I kept telling myself if I spent enough time with you,

I'd get over it. That I'd get over *you*. I didn't realize until the engagement party that I didn't want to get over you."

She frowned. "The engagement party? Then why—"

"Did I take so long to come talk to you? Because I wanted to do it right. I was having this made." He reached into his back pocket and pulled out a small black jewelry box.

Flipping it open with his thumb, he went down on one knee. "Brittney Hannon, will you marry me?"

Brittney gasped. It was the ring he'd described to the older woman. A platinum filigree ring, with a single large diamond in the center and tiny sapphires on each side.

"I'm tired of doing things halfway, Brit. If you're an all-or-nothing girl, then I want to be your all-or-nothing guy." He stood and reached for her, cupping her face in his hands, his thumbs resting along her cheeks. "You said that you were already a little in love with me. Well, then you're slower than I am, because I'm more than a little in love with you. But I'm not worried. I figure a little in love is a start. And I'm not going anywhere. If I stick around long enough, you're bound to fall even more in love with me. I can wait."

As he spoke, something tightened deep in her chest, making her feel like she couldn't breath. Like his words were wrapping themselves around her very heart and giving it a squeeze.

All her life, she'd never had anyone who was always there for her. She'd never had anyone whose love she could count one. Not her mother who'd so quickly abandoned her. Not even her father, who'd always been there, but not there. And now there was Connor, promising her a lifetime.

"Do you mean that?"

He leaned down and kissed her. Slowly, gently. When he finally lifted his head, all her doubts were gone. Of course, he'd always been a persuasive kisser.

Just in case his kiss alone wasn't enough to convince her, he said, "I do mean that. I'm not going anywhere. I'm going to be right here beside you until you believe me or fall so in love with me that you don't care."

The smile she could no longer contain broke across her face. "Are you really going to make me wait that long? Because I'm ready now."

He took her in his arms and kissed her deeply. Unlike his earlier gentle kisses, this one was tinged with the heat that had marked their first kisses. There was nothing soul-soothing or careful about him. Instead it was fierce and possessive, hungry and joyful all at the same time.

Before she knew it, his fingers had worked free the buttons of her blouse and his mouth had nudged it off her shoulder. "Thank goodness," he muttered against her skin. "Feels like I've been waiting forever to touch you again." His hands reached down to cup her bottom. He lifted her against him, and she instinctively wrapped her legs around his waist. "Please tell me I'm not going to have to debate abstinence for another hour before you'll let me touch you."

She threw her head back and laughed. "Let's talk about it in the bedroom."

With one arm supporting her weight and the other across her back, he had carried her a few steps towards her bedroom when the doorbell rang.

He quirked his eyebrow.

"Takeout, from Topaz Thai."

Connor nodded. "He can wait. I can't."

Which was just fine with Brittney. She'd been waiting for Connor her whole life.

Epilogue

Brittney Stone walked into the VIP tent of the 2011 Clearwater Media Polo tournament with her husband's hand possessively resting on the small of her back. Though her father had pushed for a big summer wedding, she and Connor had decided to have a quiet ceremony in the early spring, right on the shore of Long Pond, surrounded by the crocus blooms. Their wedding was everything she could have hoped for. Small, unpretentious and lacking the drama and scandal that had marked their early courtship. It had been a day filled with happiness and laughter.

Since returning from their honeymoon to Costa Rica, they'd been living quietly in the city. This was their first big social event as a married couple.

In the tent, she caught Vanessa's and Nicolas's eyes. The married couple waved them over enthusiastically. Brittney smiled at the sight of tiny baby Gabriella propped on Vanessa's hip. Vanessa and Nicolas had married at the end of the previous year's polo season. As they approached their first anniversary, they looked as happy as ever.

Vanessa gave Brittney a quick buss on the cheek. "Marriage must agree with you. You look fabulous."

"You, too." Brittney leaned back to give her friend an assessing stare while Nicolas greeted Connor. Nicolas and Vanessa had been traveling so much following the polo circuit, it seemed ages since Brittney had seen them. Now, she could only chuckle. "How you manage to still wear your signature white while carrying around a baby, I'll never know."

Vanessa laughed, then leaned forward and whispered, "The baby is actually the trick. She's so cute no one notices me."

"May I?" Brittney asked, with a nod toward Gabriella.

"Sure." Vanessa carefully handed the baby over to Brittney.

Holding her sturdy little body close to her chest, Brittney felt something inside her melt into goo. Gabriella swung out a chubby fist to grab a lock of Brittney's hair. Gabriella had her father's soulful eyes and her mother's sassy smile. In short, she was perfect. Even better, she was obviously surrounded by a loving family.

On the way into the tent, Brittney and Connor had run into the other members of the Hughes family. Christian, who was now semiretired and well on the road to recovery, had been holding his other grandchild, Christian Fitzgerald Hughes, showing him the polo ponies. Julia and Sebastian, who were hosting the event again this season, were near the entrance mingling with guests. Julia was clearly flourishing as the new VP of PR for Clearwater, and the expression on Sebastian's face showed just how proud he was of his wife. It was obvious to anyone who saw them that although they worked together, there was nothing businesslike about their relationship.

The Hugheses stood talking to Sheikh Adham and Sabrina, who had returned to the Hamptons to celebrate their first anniversary. Brittney had heard through the grapevine about the success of Grant Vineyards and Winery and of Adham's horse farm. More than just their businesses were flourishing. Sabrina all but glowed as she ran a hand along the top of her heavy belly. Though she looked ready to give birth any day now, it obviously hadn't slowed her down.

Since Adham's mother, younger sister and older brother had accompanied them to the States to attend the birth of the latest addition to their royal family, Sabrina was surrounded by the love of a close-knit family. Even the king pledged he'd fly over the moment she went into labor. It was obvious to anyone watching the couple together that the love affair that had blossomed between Sabrina and her desert prince during the previous season was blazing brighter every day. They were regularly providing the polo community and the paparazzi with more sensational instances of spontaneous passion.

The sheikh's family wasn't the only royalty in attendance, since the VIP tent held its share of Hollywood royalty as well. Matthew and Carmen Birmingham returned to the Hamptons this summer with their three-month-old twin sons. Everyone was convinced the little darlings were conceived the year before at the Hamptons since the couple spent a lot of time behind closed doors, and when they were seen at a polo match you could clearly see the love shining between them. Even though it was only summer and awards season was months away, Hollywood gossip was already touting the Birminghams' documentary film on the history of the Statue of Liberty as shoo-in for an Academy Award for Best Documentary Feature.

As Vanessa and Nicolas and Gabriella moved on to greet the Birminghams—and no doubt compare baby stories—Connor led Brittney over to Richard Wells and Catherine Lawson. Connor knew Richard from the city, and they'd run into the other couple socially a few times. The men immediately launched into a discussion about the polo team's season. Brittany gave Catherine a brief hug.

"You got our RSVP for the wedding, right?" she asked.

Catherine nodded. "They've been flooding in, but I definitely remember seeing yours."

Richard and Catherine had planned their wedding for the end of the season. Catherine had confided that she and Richard had both wanted to take the time to get to know each other better before the wedding. It was certainly an approach Brittney could appreciate, though it was obvious how much they adored each other.

"How's the riding school going?" Brittney asked.

Catherine's face split into a grin. "Huge success! We have plenty of students and we're making real gains with the underprivileged kids who are being sponsored to attend on weekends. Spring camp was a success, and the summer camp looks to be even better. Thanks for sponsoring some of the kids."

"It's the least I can do," Brittney said. "Just let us know when we can help again."

Catherine positively beamed. "I'm so blessed to have friends like you to support the school. In less than a year, I've gone from just dreams to a reality that's better than I could have imagined."

But Brittney knew, watching Catherine's expression, that the real blessing was Richard, whose financial guidance at the school was just the tip of the iceberg.

Richard had also succeeded in tracking down the polo team owner/patron who set Catherine's father up in a horse-doping scandal thirteen years ago. The patron's assets and horses had been seized, and he was being held in custody while under further investigation by the authorities. He looked to be facing a long time in jail for that and other illegal activities. None of that would bring Catherine's father back, but she seemed to feel he had been vindicated and his name had been publicly cleared of all scandal. Now, Brittney couldn't help noticing how happy Catherine looked. She was obviously looking forward to the next stage in her life with a light and happy heart and knew that with Richard by her side she could do and achieve anything.

After chatting a few minutes longer, Brittney and Connor headed out to the bleachers in hopes of catching a little of the match. Besides, although the social scene was fun, Brittney really just wanted to be alone with her husband.

Now, just a few months into their marriage, all her initial doubts about Connor had faded. Their love no longer felt fragile and new. He'd been true to his word. He'd shown her how much he loved her every day, in a million tiny ways. And in many not-so-little ways, she thought with a grin as her hand drifted over her belly.

She didn't know if she was pregnant—it was too soon for that—but she had hopes, and she had a husband who would be by her side no matter what. What more could a woman ask for?

* * * * *

Silhouette Desire

COMING NEXT MONTH

Available October 12, 2010

REQUEST YOUR FREE BOOKS!

2 FREE NOVELS
PLUS 2
FREE GIFTS!

Passionate, Powerful, Provocative!

SDES10R

HARLEQUIN® Romance®

MARGARET WAY

introduces

THE *Rylance* DYNASTY

The lives & loves of Australia's most powerful family

Growing up in the spotlight hasn't been easy, but the two Rylance heirs, Corin and his sister, Zara, have come of age and are ready to claim their inheritance. Though they are privileged, proud and powerful, they are about to discover that there are some things money can't buy....

Look for:

Australia's Most Eligible Bachelor

Available September

Cattle Baron Needs a Bride

Available October

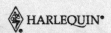